Head Cook
at Weddings and Funerals

HEAD COOK AT WEDDINGS & FUNERALS

And Other Stories Of Doukhobor Life

VI PLOTNIKOFF

Head Cook At Weddings And Funerals

Second Printing January 1995

Published by:
Polestar Press Ltd.
1011 Commercial Drive, Second Floor
Vancouver, BC
Canada V5L 3X1

The Publisher would like to acknowledge the financial assistance of The Canada Council, British Columbia Cultural Services Branch, and the Department of Canadian Heritage.

The author wishes to thank the Canada Council Explorations Program for their assistance.

Cover design and illustration by Jim Brennan.
Production by Michelle Benjamin and Julian Ross.
Edited by Rita Moir and Julian Ross.
Printed in Canada by Best-Gagne.

Canadian Cataloguing in Publication Data

Plotnikoff, Vi.
Head cook at weddings and funerals and other stories of Doukhobor life

ISBN 0-919591-75-2
I. Doukhobors — British Columbia — Fiction.
I. Title.
PS8581.L67H42 1994 C813'.54 C94-910490-6
PR9199.3P56H42 1994

Dedicated to my mother Annie Kootnekoff Makaeff and to the memory of my late father, Ignace Peter Makaeff, who wrote, sang and believed "Life is Worth Living."

And to my Doukhobor ancestors and their endless quest for peace.

The stories and characters in this book are fictitious. Historical events, culture and customs are authentic to the best of my knowledge.

Some of the stories have appeared in the following anthologies and magazines, and I would like to thank the editors: *Journey to the Interior, Osprey's Nest,* and *Wordworks.*

I wish to thank David McFadden, my former creative writing teacher who first urged me to write from my roots, and Myler Wilkinson and Vera Makaeff for their support and honesty. Also Koozma Tarasoff, Eli Popoff, Gordon Turner, Judy Wearmouth, Vi Kalesnikoff, and the Castlegar Writers Guild. Thanks to my editor Rita Moir, and my publishers Julian Ross and Michelle Benjamin. And thanks to my family: Ron, Larry, Peg, Kylie and Jill, and especially Serge.

— *Vi Plotnikoff*

Head Cook at Weddings and Funerals
and Other Stories of Doukhobor Life

Introduction

Taken together, these 14 stories mark a new departure by a writer of Doukhobor origins. Vi Plotnikoff writes from deep within her first culture; she has a profound knowledge of Doukhobor traditions and an intimate, lived experience of her people's folk customs and everyday lives. In this book, she recreates a recent past which even now is fading from cultural memory. Her images are intense and real, acting immediately on the senses: the smell of new-mown hay at midsummer, of borsch in communal kitchens; the feel of dust kicked up on still country roads and of autumn leaves drifting to the distant streets of a remembered childhood.

These stories will appeal to Doukhobor readers as complex and bittersweet images of themselves reflected back through the prism of literature. But readership will not be limited to any one cultural group. Non-Doukhobor readers of all backgrounds will be fascinated by the window these stories offer onto a unique people — the Doukhobors, or "Spirit Wrestlers", as they were named by an angry church father in eighteenth-century Russia.

The history of these people is traced in the pages of the book. We learn of the pacifist beliefs which led to the "burning of arms" in 1895 and eventual mass migration to Canada at the very end of the nineteenth century. We follow the Doukhobors through their years of homesteading on the Canadian prairie, women pulling plows in teams in order to break the virgin lands. We see the Doukhobors as they give up their lands and many of them move to the Kootenay region in British Columbia. And we watch as a zealous minority group breaks away from the large group of Doukhobors and turns to desperate acts to express its rejection of dominant cultural values.

Most Canadians will have heard the latter stories: sensational and often inaccurate media accounts, and it is this negative portrayal of the Doukhobors which Vi Plotnikoff writes against with all the force of her artistic conscience. Hers is a voice which asks for understanding and dignity for cultural difference.

In this book, we see the world through the eyes of the narrator Ana, as she grows from girlhood to young womanhood. In her struggle to deal with the pain of cultural separateness, she comes to realize that her people's past is alive within her no matter which other worlds she may inhabit in the future.

Vi Plotnikoff does not stand entirely alone; what she writes has been made possible in part by the earlier literary achievements of her own culture. But she does occupy a unique historical moment in the development of Doukhobor writing. No one else of her generation has written a fictional work of this artistic calibre, which grows out of Doukhobor experience yet reaches beyond it, with the potential to touch people of all backgrounds. This is an ambitious book, and it cannot have been an easy one to write; the author's vision takes her to the margins where cultures and generations meet.

The writing is filled with the journeys and crossings of people attempting to understand themselves in relation to worlds beyond the known and comfortable.

With wisdom and simplicity, Vi Plotnikoff's stories of Doukhobor experience portray a reality faced by Canadians as a whole: we are a people who know what it is to face cultural marginalization, a marginalization which can only be overcome by recognizing the worth of our own stories. There are many minority cultures in this country, many voices with unique stories to tell. In this volume, Vi Plotnikoff takes an important step toward that self-realization which is Doukhobor, and Canadian.

Myler Wilkinson
South Slocan
April 1994

Myler Wilkinson is a specialist in both Russian and North American literature. He has twice been a guest lecturer in Russia and currently teaches at Selkirk College in Castlegar, B.C.

Aunt Sofie and the Soldier

My Aunt Sofie was what we called stylish. Her clothes were straight out of the front pages of Eaton's catalogue, never the budget section in the middle. Aunt Sofie was papa's youngest sister and the prettiest. She had large hazel eyes, luxuriant dark brown hair upswept into a roll secured by rhinestone combs, and a tall, slim figure. My dream was to grow up to look just like Aunt Sofie.

While her friends worked in the fields in summer and stayed home in winter and filled their soondookee, their hope chests, Aunt Sofie worked as a nurse's aide in the Valley Cottage Hospital and spent her paycheque on clothes.

Aunt Sofie even changed her last name from one ending with a double "ff" to a "v". This way, no one from out of town would connect her with her ethnic origin. And she never, ever ate sunflower seeds, even though every garden had them growing in profusion and everyone we knew had them in their pockets, and consequently on the floors. The teachers at school would threaten us, "Leave them at home, or you'll get the strap." We were also threatened with the strap if we spoke Russian at school. Aunt Sofie never spoke Russian outside the house, and no one could tell she wasn't a good Anglo-Saxon girl.

Aunt Sofie's parents lived on the farm, so she stayed with us in town, crowding into our already bulging house. She shared one of the attic bedrooms with me, usually stealing in well past midnight and pushing me toward the wall with her icy feet. In the morning, mama would wake us girls for school by yelling up the stairs. I would lurch up but Aunt Sofie didn't stir. She was a mound of lightly snoring blankets. As I pulled on my scratchy wool stockings, always in the same ugly brown, I'd glance down at Aunt Sofie's gossamer heap of nylons on the floor. No matter how cold the night, she always wore nylon stockings.

"Sofie has legs like a racehorse," I once heard papa's friend say admiringly as he watched her slim, silken-clad legs with black seams parading around our tiny house.

When no one was home, my sisters and I spent many delightful hours trying on Aunt Sofie's silk blouses, her grey stride slacks and taffeta party dresses, carefully dropping the shimmering folds over our heads, then standing back to admire our skinny bodies. Sometimes we tried her makeup, the mascara and scarlet lipsticks and nail polish, even the deodorant.

Whenever baba came to visit, she brought along her standard lecture.

"Sofie, you shouldn't work in hospital, rubbing old men's backs," baba said. "You should stay home, work on soondook, embroider pillowcases, crochet doilies. What will starooshka say when she see soondook? Nothing but fancy clothes in it. She take her son home right away." Baba took another sip of tea and moved the sugar lump to the other side of her mouth. "And what man want wife who spend all his money and buy clothes and go to dances at Oddfellow Hall? No. Man want wife who cook good borsch and pirahi, grow garden, milk cow."

Aunt Sofie would roll her eyes and mutter, "I'd rather be dead," and prepare to leave the room. But not before baba gave her final parting shot.

"You going to be old maid! You already twenty-seven."

Aunt Sofie would march up the stairs, rag rollers quivering with indignation.

Baba turned to us. "Noo, devooshkee. You learn to cook?"

"Da, baba," we chorused.

"I helped mama make borsch last time," I said.

"Horosho." Good. "I teach you to mend socks. Knit mittens." I didn't dare tell her I wanted to be exactly like Aunt Sofie when I grew up.

One day when I was downtown after school, I saw Aunt Sofie in her nurse's uniform. I stopped, staring because she was in the company of a good-looking man in a soldier's uniform. He was sporting a mustache. I loved mustaches. All my Hollywood idols had them. The man was a stranger and I figured he must be in the Korean War. Our teachers told us about it at school. My family, being pacifist, was against everything military and seeing Aunt Sofie talking to a man in uniform was a shock. My father and grandparents would be furious.

I walked slowly toward Aunt Sofie and the soldier, and was about to say "hi" when Aunt Sofie saw me. She frowned, then grabbed the soldier's arm and pointed toward the shop window.

"Look, Bill. Isn't that a darling hat? Think I should buy it?"

He looked puzzled at her shrill tone, then smiled and said it would look beautiful on her. I walked on slowly, wondering why she pretended not to see me and why she should suddenly be interested in hats when she never wore one. Even in winter, when everyone else wore kerchiefs, she was bareheaded.

I came home and told mama about it. She questioned me about the soldier, then told me not to say anything to anyone. "None of your business," she said.

A couple of days later, Aunt Sofie called me into the living room where she turned down Lux Radio Theatre on the big battery radio.

"Ana, I want to talk to you." She wasn't looking at me, choosing instead to contemplate the red nails she was filing. "About the other day. I hope you didn't misunderstand. I didn't introduce you to that soldier because, well, I didn't really know him. He just stopped me on the street and started talking."

"You knew him all right. You called him 'Bill'. You just didn't want me to meet him." I was still smarting from the snub.

Aunt Sofie patted the waves on her freshly permed head.

"Well, you see, he's a soldier, and I didn't want you to tell anyone I knew him. You know how excited the people around here would get. Especially about the uniform. They'd be at me all the time. I have enough trouble about my job."

"I wouldn't have told. But you were ashamed of me. You're just as bad as the teachers. You were afraid I'd say something in Russian."

"Ana, that wasn't it."

"It was so. You changed your last name, didn't you?"

"That's my business." Aunt Sofie's face was red and I knew her famous temper had surfaced.

"I hope he finds out you're Russian and eat borsch and your relatives wear kerchiefs."

"Shut up, you little stinker."

She stood up and the latest edition of *Glamour* magazine slid to the floor.

"And while you're at it, you kids leave my clothes alone, and my magazines. Oh, don't deny it. I see the greasy pages all the time."

"And you quit pushing me into the wall every night, and wear some socks to bed. Your feet are always cold. Bill won't marry you if I tell him what cold feet you have."

She gasped and came toward me. I knew I'd gone too far and fled outdoors.

After that, an uneasy truce settled between us. We spoke only in public.

"Pardon me."

"Oh, excuse me, please."

In private, silence thundered between us. Thank goodness Aunt Sofie continued to creep home after midnight and we were spared being awake together in the double bed.

The following week, my youngest sister Lisa came home from school with a sore throat and fever. Next morning her face had flowered with red spots.

"Measles," Dr. Tenholme pronounced when he was summoned.

Two days later, Sara and I were similarly afflicted. Mama made up the big living room sofa into a double bed and added a cot. It was much warmer there with the wood heater, and closer to the kitchen. Aunt Sofie was called upon to help and she needed all her nursing talents to cope with us.

The Saturday baba came to visit was the worst day of all. We were convalescent, bored and irritable. The room was hot and messy. Baba was lecturing Aunt Sofie on her marital status. Mama had served us her special invalid soup, a vegetable concoction thickened with oatmeal, and Lisa had just spilled hers on Sara's nightie, resulting in a fight.

A knock startled us. Baba was nearest the door. She opened it and there stood the soldier. His eyes widened as he took in the kerchiefed woman in the doorway.

"Hello, hello," she said. "You look for somebody? Maybe neighbours?" You certainly don't belong here, her tone said.

"I thought ... I mean ... do you know where a Sofie lives?"

"Sofie? Why you want Sofie? How you know her?"

"Then you do know her?"

"Where you see her? Oddfellow Dance?"

"Does she live near here? Next door maybe?" he said hopefully, shifting his cap between his hands uncomfortably.

Baba turned back to Aunt Sofie, who stood unmoving, her face mirroring panic. "Sofie, you know soldier? How he know you?" She added the latter in Russian.

The soldier took in Aunt Sofie's stringy hair, her faded rose chenille robe. He looked around at the rumpled beds and us spotted children, and slid his eyes quickly past the bedpan near the door.

The silence lengthened. Baba and my sisters didn't know what was going on, but sensed something was wrong. I hardly breathed, feeling a flicker of pity for Aunt Sofie. It was the first kindly feeling I'd had for her in days.

"You girls want more soup?" mama asked as she came in from the kitchen.

With a gasp, Aunt Sofie turned and ran up the stairs. Mama looked at the soldier, then at me. I nodded. A soft "ohh" escaped from her.

"Why you want my Sofie? You see she don't want to talk. You go back. We don't want soldiers here."

The soldier didn't say anything. Just put on his cap and turned and quickly walked down the path to the street. No one spoke for a long while, then baba asked for some tea.

Aunt Sofie stayed upstairs all day, not even coming down for supper. Surprisingly, baba left her alone.

For a while, I didn't know what happened between Aunt Sofie and her soldier. Then a few weeks later, I overheard her tell mama that he was a snob from a rich family and she was glad they hadn't become serious, because he'd never understand her family's background and she was tired of concealing it. They'd parted, she said, on good terms at the Oddfellow Dance where they'd first met.

But for a long time afterwards, I heard Aunt Sofie crying softly in bed. And once, when looking through her new lingerie, I found a large colour portrait of the soldier. It was signed, "To Sofie ... Love always, Bill."

Like a Russian Duchess

I saw the braid for the first time when I was thirteen. My baba showed it to me when I was visiting the farm, and we were looking through sepia-coloured photographs with little borders around them. They were tied with red ribbon and neatly stored in packets in a large chocolates box with a picture of a woman in an old-fashioned bonnet painted on it.

"What's that?" I reached underneath the pictures, touched the small parcel of purple silk.

Baba lifted it, slowly unwrapped the silk, and laid it out on the table.

A long, thick kossa, a braid, lay there. The light from the coal-oil lamp played up the auburn lights of the most beautiful hair I'd ever seen, its glory undiminished by the years.

"Whose hair?"

"Mine. My kossa."

"But why did you cut it off?"

"I had to. We all did."

Gently she lifted the braid. Underneath lay a rainbow of ribbons, masses of silken colour, scarlet, sky blue, sunny yellow, emerald, iridescent purple.

"See, I tied my kossa with these ribbons. My mama

saved them when she sewed our blouses and zanaveski, our Sunday aprons, and if the cloth was pretty, she'd give us the scraps. My hair was thick and took so long to wash and comb. I had to braid it tight or it would spring out all around my head. My best time was when the chores were done and my padrooshki, my girlfriends and I would walk out on the prairie and play and unbraid our hair and run with the wind."

She was talking in a low voice, a smile playing around her mouth, her eyes not on the mountains outside the window, but on the windy, flat prairie of her youth.

My baba Natasha had arrived in Canada at four years of age, leaving Russia when her people were persecuted, imprisoned, exiled for refusing to serve in the military. In Canada they received homestead lands, built sod-roofed villages.

She remembered her first spring on the prairie. She'd been in her fifth year, clinging to her mama after the upheaval of the journey. Her papa left to work on the railway, along with the other men. Money was needed to buy horses, seeds.

Natasha recalled the warm sun on her kerchiefed head that soft spring day as she and her sister Loosha stood in their long, loose dresses, barefoot, listening to the talk swirling above them.

The people in the village stood looking at acres of bush and grass stretching to the horizon, waiting to be seeded.

But first the land had to be broken. Impossible without horses. And there were hundreds of people to feed throughout the summer and over the cold, dark winter.

Natasha didn't know who got the idea, but suddenly everyone was talking excitedly and several women, including her mother Polya, were helping the dedushkee, grandfathers, drag the big plough out to the field and the women began harnessing themselves to it. Twelve or fourteen women to do the work of horses. Was it possible?

Old Grisha Masloff clutched the handles, hung onto the plough as it wobbled on its side. Even Natasha could see how frail Grisha looked.

"Straighten the plough, Grisha," someone shouted. "Hold it up."

The team of women began to pull, the harness creaking and becoming taut. At first nothing happened, the blade bumping uselessly over the grass.

"Grisha. Steady. Lean on the handles."

Natasha held her breath as the blade slowly sank into the earth, caught, turned up a chunk of soil and grass amidst shouts of "tak, tak horosho." That's it, that's good.

A few minutes later, they stood looking down at the short uneven furrow of rich black soil. Even though there was still a lot of hard work ahead, they were laughing and elated. They knew there would be food on the tables that winter.

Natasha had married at sixteen. To her parents' dismay, she'd fallen in love with a young man named Dmitri, who was slight of build and whose family was a little different from the staunch Doukhobor community they lived in on the Saskatchewan prairie. Dmitri and his family, in fact all his ancestors, were horsemen in the Ukraine and Russia, and Dmitri continued this love for horses, preferring to work with a team of animals to the more mundane chores like carpentry or farming.

Natasha had met him one Sunday afternoon when she and her girlfriends were out walking across the fields after molenye, prayer meeting. Sunday was for visiting and eating, and on this beautiful June afternoon, away from their mothers' watchful eyes, they sang and danced, laughed and picked wildflowers, enjoying freedom from the drudgery of digging seneca roots to sell for medicines, from working the gardens on the unforgiving land.

"When I grow up, I'm going to Saskatoon and buy all kinds of pretty material and lace for my skirts and blouses," her friend Olya said.

"Not me," said Natasha. She'd untied the ribbon at the end of her braid, letting her long reddish hair cascade over her shoulders down to her waist in shining waves. She knew her friends were envious of her hair, the thickness, the unusual shafts of light when the sun played with it. She tossed her head sideways so her hair swung gently back and forth. Her mother told her not to be vain, but she was secretly proud, especially when everyone in the village talked about her hair.

"What's Saskatoon? It's so small. I'm going to Winnipeg and buy a long velvet coat and a hat, and pin my hair up with a big brooch in a large pouffe. Then I'll ride around the villages like a Russian duchess in my fancy phaeton and white horse with its mane and tail braided with red ribbon."

"Natasha, how wicked! And worldly."

"And I'll drive it myself."

"Oh, you're bad. May we ride with you then?"

The sun was warm on their backs, the trill and chatter of the birds almost too much for the senses. They took off sturdy shoes, long stockings, stepped carefully around gopher holes, buried hot toes in cool soft grass.

In a month or so, if the weather continued to be good, the grass would be dry and bristly, the landscape covered with dust, the wheat ripening, turning golden. But today, after the long winter, spring was overwhelming.

They were so busy chattering, they didn't see the horseman until he was quite near. He'd seen them from a distance, recognizing the long skirts and braids, the slim figures of young, single Doukhobor women. Married women wouldn't be on the prairie on a Sunday afternoon. They would be at home, preparing the big Sunday meal and minding their babies, talking to husbands they hardly had time to see all week.

Natasha looked up as he approached. A young man, but not a teenager like herself. At least twenty, possibly more. Horse and rider merged together in fluid movement, totally one, part of the prairie. Fine featured, almost-black hair and eyes. And it was his eyes she remembered that night as she lay in bed next to Loosha. The softness, the intensity of his gaze as he looked at her. He reminded her of the handsome brooding poet in one of her Russian books.

He rode up, nodded as he reined in his horse, greeted them, "Dobrai dyen, devooshkee," then galloped off. He'd looked shy, uncertain, except when he'd looked at Natasha, and his mouth had curved into a slight smile.

As she lay in the darkness, listening to her sister's slight snores — Loosha had a cold in the head, and the root teas their mother brewed hadn't helped — Natasha wished she'd smiled back instead of standing barefoot, mouth agape. She gathered he was from a neighbouring village and hoped she'd see him soon, now that she was allowed to roam around a bit with her girlfriends. In fact she was fifteen, almost marriageable age.

The following Sunday, Natasha finished her chores before molenye, much to her mother's surprise. She glanced anxiously up at the cloudy skies as she hurried to catch up to her parents and Loosha, hoping it wouldn't rain, although the wind did smell fresh.

Inside the barren meeting hall, she stood with her mother and sister, facing the men across the little table on which a large, round loaf of bread sat beside the wooden bowl of salt, and the little pitcher of water, symbols of peace and hospitality.

There was no minister, no priest. Just an old man over in the first row who began reciting a lengthy psalm in Russian. Everyone memorized psalms when they were babies, as soon as they began to say their first words. The next man began to recite, and the next, followed by the women. Natasha shifted from one foot to the other, wishing they would choose shorter psalms today of all days.

And then from the third row, Fedya Morozov began to sing the haunting melody of a psalm and everyone joined in, the voices swelling in four-part harmony, filling the little building. Fedya was a renowned zavodzhik, a starter. On key. Not too high, not too low, easy to follow.

Fedya took the hand of the man beside him, and they bowed to the spirit of God in each other, kissed and bowed again. After the men finished bowing, the women did the same.

Natasha craned her neck around the row of women behind her, trying to see out the window. Had the skies cleared? Would the handsome young man be out on the prairie today? She received a sharp poke on her arm from her mother.

"Stahyee smeerna." Stand still, Polya whispered.

Finally, finally the Lord's Prayer was being recited and as Natasha repeated the words along with everyone else, she had an unobstructed view of the window, saw the rain washing down the glass panes in great silver ribbons. As the crowd said in unison "Bohoo nashemoo slava," Glory to God, Natasha exclaimed "och nyet" in such a loud, strident voice her father at the end of the front row heard, frowned and shook his finger at her, causing everyone to turn and stare at Natasha.

She was so humiliated to be the centre of this unwanted attention that for the remainder of the molenye she looked straight ahead and enthusiastically sang the three required hymns, wondering if she could pass off her dismayed shout as a sneeze.

By the time she'd walked down the dirt road in the middle of the village and reached her house, the rain had turned into a deluge, thunder rolling and booming and lightning zig-zagging alarmingly near.

She stood inside the doorway wondering whether to cry or stamp her feet in frustration. She spent the wet afternoon helping her mother cook a big pot of borsch for supper.

To her relief, the following Sunday was hot and cloudless, and right after molenye the girls again headed for the fields. Natasha had hinted all week that the weather would be wonderful for a walk, the flowers ready for picking. She'd worried her friends would decide to visit at home instead, and she herded them down the path toward the prairie, chattering brightly.

They set off toward Tambovka village and soon met with a group of young men and women, also walking on the prairie. Natasha searched for the horseman among the boys, but when she saw him, he didn't seem as dashing as he did the first time she saw him. Small, not as romantic as he did on the horse. And then he smiled.

Everyone was shy, the boys showing off, the girls standoffish. They looked sideways at each other when they thought no one was looking. Natasha saw her cousin Verachka among the strangers and soon they were talking. The young man — Dmitri, she heard him called — was at her side, not saying much, mostly listening and staring. She didn't know whether she liked him or tall-and-handsome Vanya from her village, who never stopped talking and who all the girls wanted to walk with.

"Vanya would make a good husband. He's strong and good looking, you'll have pretty children," Natasha's mama often said.

Then came the midsummer evening Dmitri sang his song. It was late, the sun a glowing orange disc perched on the horizon, then slipping right into the ground, to the centre of the earth it seemed. The boys and girls from the two villages had become friends. No longer showing off, but pairing up, holding hands, and sometimes singing together. And then, as they stood in an uneven circle in the purpling twilight, Dmitri began to sing. Natasha had never heard the song before. It was a sad tune, the words even sadder. A farewell to the green hills, and the forests of the country of his youth, and the move to a strange new land. Natasha felt tears sting the backs of her eyes, for she'd felt the same when she'd left Russia ten years ago. She tossed her unbraided hair, pretending nonchalance.

And she knew right then who she would marry.

Warm autumn days followed the hot summer. Wheat harvested, potatoes and pumpkins and root crops stored in cellars, barrels of sauerkraut prepared.

"They're coming to get me." Natasha would say to her mother and Loosha as they dug potatoes, speaking softly so the women working behind them wouldn't hear. "Probably before the snow comes. So I don't know why I have to work so hard when I won't be living in this village."

"No," her mama would say. "You're too young to marry. Besides, Vanya is in our village. We would see you every day if you marry him." Polya dug her spade deep into the black soil, brought up a shovelful of huge tubers covered with damp earth. Natasha and Loosha quickly picked them out, threw them into buckets. Their backs ached but they dared not stop. The older women would yell at them for sure.

"I tell you, I don't want to marry Vanya," Natasha said, emptying her pail into the wagon. "Dmitri's mother and father are coming for me before the snow falls."

"Docha, please wait until spring. You'll be a little older, more sure."

Reluctantly Natasha agreed. It would be difficult to see Dmitri during the bitterly cold winter, but she could work on her soondook and spring would be around the corner. Besides, her hair would grow even longer and thicker by spring. She would be the prettiest bride in all of Saskatchewan.

It was a long winter with many blizzards. The road to Tambovka village often disappeared under drifting snow, the icicles hanging to the ground on the eaves of the houses. Natasha and Loosha rarely ventured outdoors except to molenye, spending long days and nights knitting woollen stockings and mittens, sewing pillowcases and dishtowels out of flour and sugar sacks and, in the evenings, lying atop the huge petch, the clay oven which produced the most wonderful brown loaves of bread. While warming their backsides, they learned to recite by heart yet another psalm, or listened to papa read from his book of Russian poetry by the light of the coal-oil lamp, and to the howling of the wind.

Natasha wondered if Dmitri thought of her as he cleaned the horse barns and chopped wood. What if he forgot her and the promise they'd made to marry in spring? There were lots of pretty girls in his village.

But Dimitri rode out on his horse a few times during that long winter. If it were Sunday and not snowing or blowing, he'd arrive in the afternoon and they'd sit on the bench at the table, sipping tea and eating kalachy, the large soft cookies, under her parents' watchful eyes, gently nudging their feet under the table, the only time they touched. Of course, Loosha sat beside her sister, being nosy, blushing violently whenever Dmitri spoke to her. Natasha was amused because she knew Loosha had a crush on him, this big brother and handsome young man combined. Sometimes Dmitri would stay for supper before bundling up in his tooloop, big coat, and heading out into the winter night. Natasha worried he'd miss the road in the darkness and get lost on the endless prairie, freeze to death, be found in spring after the thaw.

She was overjoyed when once again snow was melting on the eves of the houses. The road through the village became a river of mud.

"They're coming," again she began her chant, and this time her mother began making plans for the svadba, the wedding.

On a warm June afternoon, almost a year to the day since she'd seen Dmitri on the meadows, he arrived by wagon from his village, with his parents and sisters.

After the greetings, bowing to the ground to their parents, and the reciting of prayers around the bread, salt and water, best wishes were bestowed on the newlyweds by their families. Finally everyone sat down and ate borsch and bread and plov, a rice and raisin dish which was Natasha's favourite. Then, as milking time was near, Natasha's tooke, her bundle containing her worldly belongings, was thrown on the wagon and she joined her new family as they rode home in the late afternoon sun.

When she kissed her parents, her mother said in a low voice meant only for Natasha's ears, "Be a good wife, docha. Respect your new family, and your husband. And Natasha, don't wear your hair unbraided. They'll think you're too proud. Now that you're a married woman, wear a platok tied over your head."

Natasha bumped along on the front seat of the wagon, feeling conspicuous. She was among strangers now. And as she waved to friends peering at windows or in doorways, she said goodbye in her mind. To the village, to her girlfriends in whose eyes she was now zshenah, a wife, to the singing and dancing on the prairie. And goodbye especially to unbraiding her auburn hair and swinging it back and forth, delighting in the freedom.

Natasha and Dmitri shared the straw-thatched house at the end of the long street with her starichok and starooshka, Dmitri's parents, and his young sisters, Luba and Tanya. Natasha was relieved Syoma and Masha offered their tiny bedroom to the newlyweds and they themselves had moved into the large common room.

That night in the darkened little room, Natasha untied the white shawl, removed her pink wedding blouse and long navy skirt, took off her worn good shoes.

Finally she slipped the white cotton shift down over her head. She'd spent long, painstaking hours crocheting the wide lace band, sewing it onto the bodice, and she hoped Dmitri would admire it.

Natasha unbraided her hair, letting it fall to her waist, then turned toward Dmitri who'd undressed in the dark.

"You may light the lamp now," she said with a tremor in her voice.

The light bathed her creamy arms and shoulders in amber warmth, but it was her hair Dmitri was staring at.

"Maya krasaveetsah," my beauty, he whispered, putting his arms around her, burying his face in her hair. And she truly did feel beautiful.

Daytimes, Natasha tried to be a good snaha, daughter-in-law, working in the village gardens, helping Masha prepare bread to bake in the petch, washing Dmitri's clothes. For he was now her moozsh and she took over from Masha the mending and darning of his clothes, and he never complained about the crooked seams or the thick lumps she'd produced where she'd darned his woollen stockings. Nights, when the door was shut tightly between the two rooms, Natasha unbraided her hair, combing it into a shining dark curtain. Dmitri loved to stroke her hair or run his fingers through the silken strands.

"Don't ever cut it," he'd say.

"I won't, not even when it grows white."

Sundays, after molenye, they'd walk or take the wagon and visit Natasha's family and stay for the evening meal. Natasha would remove her shawl, loosen her hair as soon as they were on the prairie. It became her symbol of freedom, her one act of defiance — at least until they came to her parents' village and she hurriedly braided it.

Natasha loved those summer afternoons. Dmitri would sing his songs, usually happy or funny ones, and sometimes the sad song she'd heard him sing when she decided to marry him. She especially loved it when he would pick a small bouquet of wildflowers and present it to her.

And then Dmitri went away, joining the other men from the villages who were working on railway construction, earning money for the community. Natasha was lonely, counting the weeks until the snow fell, and he returned.

It was a brilliant October day when word came from across the country, all the way from far-off British Columbia. The sun was especially bright that day, the ground frosty where the blue and purple shadows fell on it.

It being Sunday, Dmitri's mother and sisters were at molenye. Natasha was suffering from the chills and had stayed behind, wrapped in a shawl, legs outstretched into the warm oven of the cookstove, hair streaming around her shoulders. She wished she could be out on the prairie today, running through frost-rimmed brown grass. She wished it were summer, but then it would be months until winter and Dmitri's return. She dozed.

Excited voices awakened her. Someone was crying.

She stood, shawl slipping to the floor. Was it an accident? Dmitri? Or his father? Maybe her father?

The door opened and Dmitri's sisters entered. Luba was crying.

"Never, ever. I won't."

"Me either." Tanya, the quiet one, shouted.

Not an accident. Relief made her weak.

"What's wrong?"

"Oh Natasha ..." Masha looked agitated.

It was an accident. Fear snaked through her body.

"Word has been received ..."

"Yes?"

"From British Columbia." Masha began taking off her outergarment, replenishing the woodstove. Natasha waited. She knew it wasn't an accident on the railway. But why were the girls so upset?

Masha put a small pot of bean soup on the stove, began cutting thick slices of crusty fragrant bread.

"Yes?" Natasha thought she would scream from the waiting.

"Our leader in British Columbia has decided ... all women and girls ..."

Were all women and girls being shipped back to Russia? Or being moved out west? Why else was everyone so upset?

"All women and girls must have their hair cut."

Natasha felt both relief and horror.

Luba and Tanya cried harder.

"Everyone. For sanitary reasons. It's neater when you cook. Easier to wash, keep clean." Masha avoided looking at Natasha's glorious hair cascading around her face.

"Not I," said Natasha. "I'll go to my mother's village."

"They're cutting their hair, too."

Natasha looked around wildly. She'd escape to the prairie. She'd live with the Angleekee until Dmitri returned. They'd homestead alone, away from the community.

But maybe it wasn't as bad as she thought. Hair did grow quickly. In a year or so ...

"Short, like the men's," Luba was sobbing.

"Shaved right off," Tanya said, joining in the wailing.

"No." Dmitri loved her hair more than anything. It was her most prized possession. She'd be ugly without it.

"Old Vasya is going to cut it with his barber's tools. He's been doing it for years for the men," said Masha, bringing out sauerkraut and some homemade cheese. She sounded calm, but her hands were shaking.

"When."

"Today. He's coming here today. It must be done soon."

Natasha ran to the bedroom, threw off the shawl, frantically began braiding her hair as if to protect it. If she hurried, she'd be out of the house before old Vasya arrived, running across the prairie to her mother's house.

A pounding on the door froze her movements, stayed her shaking hands. She backed up, felt the hard edge of the wooden bed against the backs of her legs. Voices exploded in the kitchen. Cries. Her starooshka's calm voice.

"Natasha." She was rooted to the floor. What if she climbed out the narrow window and ran away? Would she ever live in the Doukhobor Community again? Or worse, would Dmitri stay in the village without her? She turned, made her way to the door.

"I am ready."

Natasha pulled the shawl over her head, tying the ends neatly under her chin. In the tiny, wavy mirror her thin face stared back at her. "Rodent" she thought, looking at the spikey reddish hair under the peak of the mud-coloured shawl. It had been two weeks since the massacre, as she called it, and still she wasn't used to the feel of her bristly head.

Masha who was first, smiled weakly, looking brave for the girls' sake. Her two daughters cried and held onto each other. When her turn came, Natasha looked straight ahead, didn't utter a sound as Vasya clutched the braid in one hand, scissors in the other. To her dying day, she'd hear the terrible grinding sound of the scissors, the whack of the braid as it dropped to the floor.

Natasha picked up the braid and, looking at no one, walked into the bedroom, staying there until the next morning.

"You hurt, docha," her mother had said the following Sunday when she visited Natasha, "because you were too proud of your hair. It's what you are inside that's important."

"You don't understand," Natasha was inconsolable.

Natasha turned away from the unforgiving mirror, to the window, staring out at snow-dusted fields. Dmitri was coming home. She was happy, until a chill came over her like the cold Assiniboine. What would he think when he saw her pinched face under the shawl? It was small consolation that all the women in all the villages, from the old babushkas to the young girls, now had the same hairdo. Even the little girls, doll-like in their long dresses and kerchiefs, were shorn. The men, on their way home from weeks of living in work camps, would have an unpleasant surprise.

Nearly dusk. A curtain of light snow hung across the prairie, when out of the dimness a shadowy horseman emerged. Natasha stared out the window of her bedroom as more riders and horses appeared, then a whole convoy of wagons, horses and men with bundles rode through the curtain. The first horseman broke into a long gallop, and thundered into the village.

Natasha ran into the common room, where the others were cooking, pulled her shawl well down her forehead and opened the door, letting in a blast of frigid wind. And then Dmitri was enveloping her in his snowy arms, his icy cheek against hers. In the happiness of that moment, she still remembered to hold onto the shawl with one hand.

Syoma had soon followed his son into the little house, dropping his bundle of clothing near the door. Father and son sat at the table, where the coal-oil lamp cast an orange glow on the thin, weathered faces of the men, mercifully hiding the secrets of the four women.

"Nothing like your cooking, Masha." Syoma was ravenous, breaking sooharee, dried bread, into his soup.

"You'd think those camp cooks fed you boiled water," Masha smiled. She too kept in the shadows. No one wanted to be the first to reveal their secret.

Natasha, in her long, white flannel nightgown, the mud-colored shawl still around her head, sat on the edge of the bed, waiting for Dmitri to blow out the lamp.

"That is the ugliest shawl. Aren't you going to take it off even to sleep?"

"I'm cold." Natasha shivered.

"I want to stroke your hair ... see the lamplight shining on it."

Natasha was silent, listening to the spit and crackle of the wood stove in the next room, the soft hiss of dry prairie snow swirling against the window, the sad moaning of the wind.

For a long moment, she was like stone. Then she looked at Dmitri, and reached up and slowly pulled off the shawl, dropping it to the floor.

"Baba," I said, pulling her back to the present, "Why did you let them cut it off?"

"We did what we had to do."

"And what did deda say when he saw your hair?"

"He was surprised and sad when he first saw it, but I think I was more upset than he, for I'd been so vain about it. And even though my hair grew long and thick again, I became a mother soon afterwards and left my girlhood behind. I had more important things to think about." She paused, then added, "But I never felt really beautiful again."

Where the Streets are Paved with Gold

"Please." The tap on the screen door disturbed the slumberous afternoon heat. "Please can you help."

I stared at the small woman on the porch. At the perspiring red face and the grey-streaked black hair escaping from the bun, and I wondered how she could stand the heat in the full skirt and long-sleeved blouse. Why didn't she dress Canadian in this weather?

"Mrs. Demenoff, come in. I'll get my mother."

"She's gone. My Lily's run away!" She began to cry as my mother came into the room. "Took her good clothes and suitcase and guitar. "O Bozshi moi, Oh my God ... What will I do? I have to bring her back." Tears formed at the corners of her eyes and trickled down her brown cheeks, mixing with the sweat.

"Sit down, Molly. I'll make tea."

"She end up on Cordova Street."

We'd all heard of Cordova in downtown Vancouver. The wildest and scariest place on earth. Pimps and prostitutes, drunks, drug addicts. Never go there at night. Even daytime was scary. You had to be careful when you shopped at Army and Navy.

And now Lily from across the field walked that

frightening stretch of pavement. I was entranced.

"How do you know she went to Vancouver?" Mama said, patting the thin shoulder. "Maybe she went the other way to visit relatives."

"Nyet, she pack right in front of me. Getting free ride all the way to Vancouver just for the company, with salesman she meet waitressing. He say he get her job at brother's café right downtown. Say she could be star in big city. If only her father were here."

"She's eighteen, Molly. You can't make her come back."

As I watched Molly, head bent, walk back to her little unpainted house across the stubbly hayfield, grasshoppers leaping and clacking in her path, I rememberd a wet spring evening a couple of months earlier.

Sounds of the calliope filled the night sky before we even saw the sparkly lights of the ferris wheel, smelled the onions and cotton candy. We watched milk bottles being knocked off with a ball. Hit three and you win a long-legged kewpie doll with feathers and a grinning painted face.

Screams rose from the tilt-a-whirl and I turned away, for I'd thrown up in the weeds behind the tents last year after I'd stumbled off the whirling, tilting platform. A thin bored-looking man showed off two sleepy reptiles, "ferocious cobras from the jungles of Brazil only a quarter for the show." And on a small stage in front of a tawdry-looking tent a man with rhinestones on his shirt yelled "The best entertainers anywhere. Come in and hear them sing or dance. Anything your heart desires. They aim to please. Only one buck." We stared at the row of girls in satin dresses, flowers in their frizzy hair, cheeks feverish with rouge. They were all chewing gum.

"Look," my sister Sara pointed, "It's Lily. She's climbing up on stage. Is she going to dance?"

"She's a singer. Don't you know that? She sings at all the weddings, and does solos at sobranye when she's in the mood."

Red-haired, creamy-skinned Lily from across the field, restless and pretty, forever humming Patsy Cline songs. Quit school at fifteen. Her bedroom plastered with pictures of cowboy singers. Did nothing but moon around the house, listening to the radio, or fixing her hair as she smiled in the mirror, her mother said.

"Got her father's red hair and good looks. He could sing too, and play accordian. Best looking man around, but didn't like to work. Probably still doesn't." Then she'd added, shaking her head, "What good is strumming guitar when you don't know how to knit socks? Nice Doukhobor girls don't play instrument. They sing in choir."

Lily said something to the rhinestone man and pointed to her guitar.

He shrugged, said "why not," and she faced the small group in front of the stage. Her mother would kill her if she saw how low she was wearing her peasant blouse.

"Folks, I give you a future singing star. You can say you saw her first at Dreamland Carnivals. Your very own local talent, Miss Lily. Take it away, honey."

Lily strummed a few chords. She looked a bit scared, sang a verse of "Your Cheatin' Heart," then announced, "This next one's my own composition, 'Streets are Paved with Gold'," and she closed her eyes and sang a real sticky song about a girl who runs away to the big city and becomes rich and famous and finds her true love on Cordova Street. I didn't like it much, but her voice sounded a bit like Patsy's, or maybe it was the hairdo. The crowd cheered and whistled and Lily looked real proud.

And now she'd run away and soon would be heard on the radio.

The day after Molly's visit, I accompanied my mother to the little house in the middle of the sunbaked field. I didn't blame Lily for wanting to escape the neat, painfully bare, hot rooms. The dirt yard with the vegetable garden, the cow, and the outhouse, a smelly sentinel in the dry field. And the loneliest, most desolate sound in the world in my estimation — the sighing of the hot wind in the scrub pine behind the house.

But most of all I was glad she'd escaped her mother. And for the first time I was thankful for my sisters because my mother's love was divided among us, not possessively focussed.

I sat on the back stoop and listened to mama and Molly through the open door. I heard Molly's sniffles and occasional sobs and mama's comforting words, and thought how lucky Lily was to be in Vancouver. And how safe despite the dangers, because Molly would never go there to drag her home.

So we were all surprised when Tony over at the Stargate Café and Bus Depot told my father that Molly had got on the bus to Vancouver with her shopping bag luggage, taking the night run because it was cheaper.

"Bringing my girl home," she'd said. "Even if it takes the rest of my life."

"Bundled up, she was, in her Doukhobor clothes. Die of heat stroke on that hot bus," said Tony.

I could imagine Lily on wild and wonderful Cordova Street, encountering her mother in her voluminous outfit.

"Molly's come home," Papa said a few days later. "I saw her with her big shopping bag." That evening she came across the field and told us that Vancouver was huge and frightening and full of sin. The streets paved not with gold, but drunks who spit and called out evil things, women who staggered out of stinking beer parlours, smoking and swearing and, perhaps the most frightening thing of all, well-dressed people looking through you with cold eyes. No one spoke. No one smiled.

She'd arrived in Vancouver as the sun rose, after a bone-jarring ride through the mountains. She'd eaten her sandwiches, watching other passengers covertly. Dozed between names on the map. Osoyoos. Hope. Chilliwack. Eavesdropped as Mel the driver flirted with the girl beside her, and prayed the salesman Lily had gone with was a nice man. Molly had never gone out with an Angleek and for the first time was glad Lily's father wasn't around to see his headstrong daughter.

Molly saw the police sign on the building. Worry had made her bold and she'd walked in and told the man at the desk she was looking for her daughter. He'd laughed at her. "You wanna know how many girls named Lily live here? Kids from the interior come by the dozen, disappear between the cracks. Go home, lady. You'll hear from her sooner or later."

"You don't have daughter. You don't know," she'd yelled. The first time in her life she'd yelled at anyone.

At a sleazy café on East Hastings she spent fifty cents on a bowl of soup, trying to assess its contents as she ate. She finished the barely warm green liquid, feeling revived, the rumbling in her stomach gone. It was then that she got the idea of checking all the eating places in the city.

She walked into every greasy spoon she came across and even ventured over to the west side where the nicer places were, but no one had heard of a waitress named Lily. Nights she went to the bus depot, stretching out on a bench, bag under her head, thankful the janitor ignored her. It was in the White Rose Café on East Pender where she finally found her daughter.

The lunch hour rush was on, the steamy café jammed. As Molly stood in the doorway, she saw Lily come through the kitchen door, swinging her hips, carrying a tray of hamburgers and soup.

Molly's heart leaped with joy. "Lily. Docha," and she started toward her, but stopped as Lily's shocked eyes met hers.

"Mama, what are you doing here?"

"I've come to take you home. I've looked and looked."

"I'm not going back."

"You don't belong here. You come home. I have money for ticket."

"Didn't you hear? I'm not going back. Ever. I have to go now. My customers are waiting." She tossed her red mop of hair and brushed past her mother, almost knocking her over.

"You come home, Lily," Molly was angry. People stared at the funny little woman in the long skirt, the flowered kerchief.

Lily turned. "I'm never going back to that dump. Everyone here snickers when I tell them where I'm from. And then you come here wearing those clothes. Go away. I don't want to see you for a long time." She marched back into the kitchen, still gripping the tray.

Molly had walked out into the crowded street and made her way back to the depot. She caught the bus that night and stared dry-eyed into the darkness as the bus groaned its way back through the mountains, and she wondered if a decent Doukhobor boy would ever look at her daughter again.

"What will you do, Molly?" my mother said, passing a teacup and plate of kalachy.

"I don't give up easy," Molly said, pouring tea in her saucer to cool it, then sipping with little slurping noises. "You know, my mother, she widowed. Have eight children and we all hungry. She walk five miles with sack of wheat on her back to feed us. I lots like her. I don't give up — not til I die."

A few days later mama said, "Ana, Molly wants you to help her write a letter to Lily," and I made my way to the bare little house.

"Tell her 'come home'," Molly said when I was seated at the oilcloth-covered table. "Write that I miss her ... don't feel so good. Have pain in heart."

I dutifully wrote everything down and addressed the envelope to the White Rose Café.

I wrote several letters for Molly that hot summer. They were never answered. And still the pain in her heart didn't go away. By the time September arrived, she wouldn't leave her bed, just lay under the quilt, face pale, breathing heavily.

Dr. Tenholme prescribed brown, vile-smelling heart medicine and visited her twice a week. She wouldn't hear of going to hospital — "never come back once you're there."

Mama made borsch and took it over but Molly refused to eat, just turned her eyes toward the pine in the window.

"Wasting away," mama said, "Dying of heartbreak," and called in old Bapka Hrooshkin to ward off bad luck and restore good health with her whispered prayers and special poultices.

But Molly continued to decline.

"I'll place a telephone call to Vancouver from the co-op," Papa said one evening over supper. "See if I can reach Lily at that café. Let her know what's happening at home."

But I thought I'd already smelled death, sweet and suffocating, in the little house, heard it in the sighing of the big pine, and knew it was too late.

"She's coming home," my father said a few days later. "I called her at the café, said her mother wasn't well. She didn't say anything for a long time. I heard car horns and a siren and laughter. I said 'do you hear me Lily? Your mother's bedridden, not eating. Doctor says maybe it's her heart. Better get home before it's too late.' And she says, 'Are you sure she's not pretending ... You know, to get me to come home?' I could not believe she said that. I felt like giving her a real scolding. Soochonka, little hussy. But I just said, 'If you don't come home real soon, you'll never see your mother again,' and she says 'Okay, I guess I should then.' Real businesslike. No tears. Nothing."

"Hardly eats," mama said, "Arms thin as Lisa's here. Eyes sunk right into her skull. Just sips tea and looks out the window and says the old pine's blocking the sun. I couldn't tell her the sun was shining right into the room."

Papa got up and went out to milk Molly's cow, followed by mama carrying a small pot of vegetable soup. She would stay the evening, when another neighbour would take over.

I sat on the old trunk in Molly's bedroom, watching mama tidy up. I knew the trunk contained Molly's finest handiwork, exquisitely tucked blouses, delicately embroidered headshawls trimmed with handknotted silken fringes. They were worn only for sobranye and weddings and for the most important, most final occasion of all, one's own funeral. Molly had prepared her funeral clothes several years ago, as did most of the ladies when they felt their bones getting old and the blood in their veins growing thin, and heard the blowing of the north wind.

She'd proudly taken out the bundle last year to show mama, unwrapping layers of tissue paper to reveal palest blue and white clothing. There was even a handkerchief to hold in her folded hands, and warm bedroom slippers. It was a fine outfit in which to spend eternity.

It looked like Molly would soon be wearing it. All she would need was a pine homemade coffin.

That evening a red-haired girl got off the bus with her suitcase and guitar. She caught a ride with a passing farmer and walked across the field past our place.

"She's come home," I hollered, running inside.

"Just in time to see her mother die," mama said.

"Leave them be," said papa. "Let them sort it out."

"There's not much time," said mother. "Poor Lily, she'll be sorry someday. Death is forever."

We left them alone to make their peace. When the time came, everyone would help out, making borsch and lapsha for the meal after the funeral.

We waited for Lily's call. It never came.

"I'm going to see how Molly is. Maybe she's already gone and that girl didn't let us know. Or maybe Lily's run away again," mama said two days later.

She marched across the field and I ran to keep up. She knocked on the door.

"Lily, it's me. Open up. Lily, are you there?"

We could hear the radio somewhere in the house. No, it was Lily singing "Streets Are Paved With Gold", strumming her guitar. We looked at each other. Was Lily singing to her dying or dead mother?

Mama turned the knob, pushed at the unpainted door, and we walked in.

Morning sunlight burst through the kitchen window, lighting up the worn linoleum, the black woodstove, touching the hair of the girl sitting at the table. There was a look of sadness and resignation on her face as she sang in a soft voice.

We froze in the doorway. Finally she looked up and a defiant and embarrassed look came over her face.

"You've come to see my mother."

"Is she ...? How is she?" Mama couldn't go on. I waited, heart pounding.

Lily got up, put her guitar carefully on the table, went toward the bedroom and opened the door. Would Molly be on her deathbed, body stiffening in the final sleep?

"Come in," said a surprisingly strong voice from inside the room. I strained to see over mama's shoulder. Molly sat on the edge of the bed, fully dressed down to her old slippers, eating porridge. For a moment my mother was speechless.

"Molly, thank God. We'd given up on you for sure."

"I have miracle. My daughter come home. Doctor say I need miracle and I get one. Now got big appetite. Pain here gone." She patted her chest in the general direction of her heart. "Doctor say couple weeks I be fine. My girl, she take care of me." She smiled, radiating happiness. It was the first smile we'd seen since Lily's escape to freedom.

I glanced over at Lily as we left the house, but she

didn't meet our eyes, just said "Bye. See you soon," in a flat voice.

And as we crossed the sunbaked field, and heard the wind blowing through the pine, I heard an even lonelier sound. It was the sound of Lily's song.

The Last Rose

The letter arrived one blue twilit February afternoon. Mama had it spread out on the kitchen table when we came in from school — chilly, noses runny, starving.

"Eat," she said, putting out bread and Roger's Golden Syrup. "Oh, by the way, that letter's from my Aunt Polly near Prince Albert. She's coming for a visit. Arriving on Wednesday by train, it says."

"But where will she sleep?"

"With you, Ana. You have the big double bed and your own bedroom."

"Does Aunt Polly have children?"

"No, she was married for a short time when I was your age, but she didn't get the chance to have a family because her husband died."

"How did it happen?" I asked.

"Their horses got spooked by a small animal one night. A fox, I think it was. Anyway, they bolted and just took off and her husband couldn't do anything. And then the sleigh overturned and they were both dragged underneath it for a while and when the horses stopped — he was dead, and Aunt Polly was unconscious. She lay there in the freezing cold for nearly an hour and it's a good thing the sleigh was over her to protect her from frostbite because it sure gets cold in Saskatchewan."

"How did she get out?" Sara said, bread and syrup forgotten.

"Their neighbours came along, thank goodness, and found them, but she'd broken her leg real bad and the kostaprav, the bonesetter, didn't set it right, so she was left with a terrible limp."

"How long is she staying?"

"Until summer."

"Gee whiz. That's a long time. I won't have any privacy."

"She doesn't have much family left. She's very lonely so I want you to be polite and friendly."

Wednesday afternoon, we stood on the platform watching the engine, spewing black soot, puff up to the station. A gaunt figure got off the train and walked through the steam, leaning on a cane. As mama hugged her, we stared at the black hair with the wing of white springing from the forehead, at the kerchief covering her head, the long black coat and especially at the lame leg with the built-up heel. She reminded me of the tall, lean crow with an injured leg I'd once seen. Shrewd black eyes pierced us.

"These are your girls?" Her voice was surprisingly low, not harsh like her appearance.

"Welcome, Aunt Polly," we said in unison. We'd been practising.

That night, I lay in bed and listened as Aunt Polly dragged up the stairs. First the tap of the cane. Then the good leg. And slowly the thump of the bad one.

"I have to listen to this for three whole months," I thought as I curled up into a tight ball and pushed my body against the wall.

I heard the rustling of garments, heavy shoes softly

dropped, and finally, the sound I'd been dreading, the lowering of a body onto the bed. She lay well over on her side, a wide gap between us, the blanket pulled tight. I evened out my breathing, pretending to be asleep, hoping she wouldn't talk. I could smell the faint mustiness of her body, the scent of camphor. Finally, I slept.

In the following weeks mama and Aunt Polly talked, visited with relatives and consumed endless cups of tea. Sara, Lisa and I were uncomfortable with Aunt Polly, as she was with us. It was obvious she wasn't familiar with the ways of children.

Some mornings, I awoke to see Aunt Polly sitting on the edge of the bed, pulling on heavy cotton stockings, her bad leg crooked and pale, blue-veined, and covered in bristly black hair, the toenails yellowed. I watched as she pulled on her long dark skirt and sensible blouse over the cotton petticoat, then expertly braided her black hair into a single plait and tied on the kerchief. If she turned my way, I closed my eyes and pretended to be asleep.

At school we were preparing for Visitors' Day. Our teacher Mrs. Chalmers, who was very thin and at least six feet tall with no hips, and a twitch in the shoulders rumoured to be the result of being struck by lightning, assigned us special jobs.

"Joanie," she said to her plump, ringletted niece, "You'll be tea pourer."

"Ana and Keiko, you will pass out the teacups and cakes, and everyone will introduce their parents and friends." I was surprised because I was usually on the clean-up committee.

Keiko and I smiled at each other, pleased to be chosen together. She had been a baby when her family, along with the other Japanese families, had been forced to move from the west coast into the interior during the war because the government thought they were a threat. Many had remained in our valley. At first I'd stared at Keiko and her friends because they looked like no one I'd ever seen before. They were quiet and polite, usually sitting together in pairs or little groups. Keiko and I didn't like softball, and one afternoon, while the rest of the class was out in the ball field, our teacher had us clean blackboards instead. We beat the soft striped brushes against the brick walls of the school, smiling at each other, watching the puffs of chalk float around in the warm autumn air. The next day I'd chosen her as my partner for our social studies project. We had to build salt, flour and water maps of South America, and as we mixed and measured and worked the dough with our hands, sleeves rolled up, we became friends. She'd been shy, trying to fit in, just like I was. That had been two years ago.

At home, mama showed me how to carry a cup and saucer properly, to smile and nod as I passed it.

"Watch your feet, Ana. You know you trip over everything."

Aunt Polly sat at the kitchen table. She was knitting me a sweater.

"Maybe if I hurry, I'll have it ready for Visitors' Day," she said.

Long after everyone was in bed, and the house perfectly still except for the crackling of the woodstove and the ticking of the big clock in the living room, I could make out the faint click of knitting needles downstairs. After I was asleep, the approaching thumps on the staircase would waken me for a moment.

"Go back to sleep, Ana. It's only me."

Sometimes I'd catch Aunt Polly watching us girls as we did dishes, or peeled potatoes, and I'd get clumsy, drop the dishcloth or the paring knife. It wasn't that she was critical like Aunt Florence, it was just her eyes, that seemed to see right into my soul.

"The Last Rose," I said one day to Sara. We were out on the road in front of the house, skipping rope. Our bouncing feet made soft muddy patches on barely thawed ground. "That's what we'll call her, you know, after the song."

"What song?"

"The one we're learning at school. About an old faded rose. ''Tis the last rose of summer left blooming alone. All her lovely companions are faded and gone.'"

"Don't let mama hear you."

"Or Aunt Polly. She'll drill me with her black eyes."

The song became a game. We'd be doing homework at the kitchen table, and one of us would start humming, roll our eyes over at Aunt Polly, then giggle and whisper. Mama and Aunt Polly never noticed. They were too busy discussing deda's arthritis, or Uncle Afanasya's heart condition, and whether the family had done the right thing moving to British Columbia with the more devout Doukhobors, while the rest of the relatives had decided to stay and farm in Saskatchewan.

At school, Mrs. Chalmers had us clean and dust the classroom. "Make sure there are no sunflower seeds on the floors," or "tidy your desks in case your mothers want to look inside."

We spent long hours practising the new song, "Tis the Last Rose of Summer" featured on CBC's School Music Program, which we sang enthusiastically and off-key.

"I'm wearing a brand-new dress, red polished cotton, the newest style," said Joanie, queen of the town kids. "I hope you two are going to look nice and not embarrass me."

"Maybe I'll wear my barn clothes," I said, "What will you wear, Keiko?"

"Oh, my mother's sewing me something." Keiko's voice was polite, her eyes downcast. I couldn't tell what she was thinking.

Finally, Visitors Day arrived, and I put on my new sweater, dyed a soft pink, and showed it off.

"Thank your Aunt Polly properly," mama urged, giving me a little push.

"Thank you very much for the lovely sweater, Aunt Polly." I leaned forward and brushed my lips against the papery cheek.

"You had to kiss 'The Rose'," Sara said as we walked to school.

"Mama made me. Besides, she knit me this sweater. I'm sure glad she's visiting Aunt Florence today. I'd die if she came to school for the tea."

By early afternoon the first mothers began straggling in, dressed in Sunday best, dragging younger brothers and sisters by the hand, sitting on chairs at the back of the room. Mrs. Chalmers asked us easy questions and we all raised our arms and waved. I wished mama would get here so she could see how many questions I answered. Joanie's mother and her friends arrived in pretty dresses and hats. One wore a velvet turban which swayed precariously, and which I thought was especially charming. Sometimes I wished my mother wore hats instead of always kerchiefs in winter and shawls for sobranye. The ladies sat down amidst a cloud of perfume.

A small Japanese woman came in with two little children and the tiniest, oldest man I'd ever seen. Keiko's family.

I was proud of my mother because she was pretty and young looking and I wished she'd hurry so I could show her off. Finally the door opened and she came in and I turned right around and gave her a wide smile. Then, to my horror, Aunt Polly limped into the room. She wore her ugly black coat and the black kerchief with the large red roses and beneath it the braid hung down her back like a long thin snake. But the very worst thing of all was the tap of the cane and the thump of her leg.

At that moment, we were singing "Last Rose of Summer" for the visitors.

"All her lovely companions are faded ..." We held the high note for a long moment ... stopped ... stared at Aunt Polly. In the silence, laughter rippled from the next classroom and our tea kettle bubbled.

"And gone!" Mrs. Chalmers shouted, finally finishing the song and startling everyone.

Mama and Aunt Polly sat down and looked around, found me and smiled. I slid down in my seat, wishing I could disappear. I'd never forgive my mother for this humiliation.

I kept my eyes averted from Aunt Polly who sat awkwardly on the little chair, her twisted leg with its thick shoe stretched out sideways.

Joanie sat at the table behind the teapots, smiling and tossing her curls. She kept looking from Aunt Polly to me. Did she guess we were related?

As we passed out cupcakes and tea — "Sugar? One lump? Two? Cream, Mrs. Brown?" I was aware of curious eyes on Keiko and me.

A crash. The murmurs froze. The tea-laden air stilled.

Joanie lay on the floor where she'd tripped over Aunt Polly's cane. Mrs. Chalmers rushed over to help, her shoulders twitching, running her hands down non-existent hips.

"Sorry." Aunt Polly leaned over, picked up the cane. "I'm very sorry." She looked more like a crow than ever.

Joanie pulled at her red skirts, trying in vain to cover her plump white thighs. We caught a glimpse of lace-edged panties as Mrs. Chalmers put her hands underneath Joanie's arms from behind and pulled her up. A few of the boys snickered.

Redfaced, again behind the tea table, Joanie glared at me.

"Is she your relative, Ana? You sure look like her."

Several girls nodded in agreement, curls bobbing.

I hated them all. Even more than I hated Mrs. Chalmers with her remarks about us Russian kids and sunflower seeds. But not as much as I hated Aunt Polly.

I didn't look at my mother as I carefully arranged the pink and white cupcakes on my tray. I noticed the icing was getting runny in the overheated air, then chose the opposite side of the room and served the English ladies, as we called everyone who wasn't Russian or Japanese.

"Class." Mrs. Chalmers was tapping her pointer lightly on the desk for attention. Most of the class had felt that pointer on our knuckles and not too gently. "Now we'll introduce our families."

Oh no, I thought, I can't introduce Aunt Polly. Maybe I should be excused and go to the washroom for a while. Or maybe the fire drill bell will go off and I'll be saved.

Mrs. Chalmers pointed her stick up and down the rows and, if any of the students had visitors, they stood up and introduced them. The pointer reached my row. Down the row, closer and closer it came. I felt my hands get sweaty, my throat close.

"Your turn," the pointer waved at me.

I stood beside my desk and looked down at my shoes.

"I ... I want you to meet my mother," and then I sat down quickly. Mama stood up, nodded and smiled, sat down and looked expectantly at me.

"Ana," Mrs. Chalmer's voice. "Please introduce the lady with your mother."

Oh, nightmare of horrors. What shall I do? How could I say that the woman with the crooked leg and the long black braid was my great-aunt?

"She ..." I cleared my throat, gathering my thoughts. "She is from Saskatchewan, quite far away. Prince Albert. It's a big town actually. Much bigger than our town."

"Who is she, Ana? What is her name?"

"Polly. Her name is Polly and she is a lady." Couldn't Mrs. Chalmers see that?

"Is she your grandma?" Joanie's voice.

"No. Of course not."

"This is my Aunt Polly," came my mother's firm voice. "And she's visiting us."

"Next." The pointer, having done its damage, continued down the row. "Keiko?"

Eyes swivelled toward the strange little group near the door. The quiet children, the small woman and the wrinkled man.

"This is my mother and my grandfather and my brothers," Keiko said in a low but distinct voice, and sat down.

Of course Keiko had to say they were related. They were the only other Japanese people there. If mama hadn't spoken up, no one would have known that the ugly crow with the cane was my family.

I'll run away from home, I thought. Just keep going until I reach Osoyoos. No one will ever find me there.

Visitors Day mercifully ground to a halt. The guests left, the chairs and tea things were put away, the remaining cupcakes devoured.

"Your aunt sure looks like you," I heard Joanie and her friends call out. They laughed and ran off, leaving me on the sidewalk, deciding whether to run away or go home and face everyone, and wondering why no one teased Keiko about her family.

The house smelled with apples and spice. Mama and Aunt Polly were in the kitchen baking tarts, and I took a deep breath as I went in. They said hello and Visitors Day was interesting and did we forget the words to our song? Never mind, it still sounded fine, except for Mrs. Chalmers yelling out the last words. Didn't she ever have a loud voice? Maybe they hadn't noticed what I'd done.

All through supper I didn't look Aunt Polly in the eye, but I caught my mother looking over at me and I could tell she wasn't pleased. I went upstairs early, determined to be asleep before the thumps on the staircase began.

Something woke me. The wind? No, it was a soft humming. I lay in limbo between sleep and wakefulness thinking it was probably a dream. Then I heard it again, ever so faintly in the dark. It sounded a little like "The Last Rose of Summer" sung in a rusty voice.

I could just make out the gaunt shape in the white nightgown, the hair unbraided, falling to the waist. She was outlined against the window, looking out into the night.

I must have made a sound even though I lay perfectly still. Her voice crackled, stopped abruptly.

"Ana," the word was low, tear-filled, "I'm sorry I woke you. Go back to sleep."

I'd seen her soul, naked in the dark, and I knew I was responsible for the tears, yet not fully. There was something else. I didn't know whether to speak or pretend sleep.

"Ana, I'm sorry I caused you shame today. I shouldn't have gone ... an old cripple like me. But your mama asked, and I wanted to see you girls on your big day. That woman shouldn't have made you introduce me, then keep on and on about it."

She was blaming herself. I couldn't believe it. Not after what I'd done.

"It's okay. It was my fault. Keiko wasn't ashamed."

"Did you know 'The Last Rose of Summer' was my favourite song a long time ago? My husband used to laugh at me because I was always singing it. I too learned it at school. Did you know we used to go dancing? Every time there was a Ukrainian wedding, we'd be the last to go home."

I didn't reply. She wouldn't have heard me anyway.

"I was with child you know, when we had the accident. It was a girl. I guess I wasn't meant to have her."

I didn't know how to answer her and didn't know whether she expected one. And then it came to me. An idea born out of her loneliness and despair and my shame. Very softly I began singing "The Last Rose of Summer" and, after a long moment, Aunt Polly joined in.

Waiting for Sonya

"To sing is the ultimate joy." The man's voice choked with emotion. "To send one's song soaring over valleys and hills until it reaches the mountaintops then ascends to the skies to become one with some universal choir. It is a joy like no other, and I want you to experience it. You, and you, and especially you."

His shaking finger pointed at me. His face was flushed. Lank greying hair flopped over his eyes. He loosened his tie, wiped his perspiring face.

"I want you to sing from the heart. Intertwine your voices in melody so your audience will cry."

He reached for the songbook, leafed through dog-eared pages. "Now try this one. It lends itself magnificently to a trio of girls' voices. Young and innocent."

He opened his collar button, took a deep breath. "I'll sing it and you try to visualize the steppes of Russia and the majestic Don River. Think of young women dancing in blossoming cherry orchards or among the graceful shivering birch trees."

Zina and Marion and I looked at each other in embarrassment. We'd come to learn to sing, not listen to a homesick man pining for his long lost homeland. Didn't he know this was Canada, the most beautiful place on earth?

It was rumoured Andrei Ramirov had been a teacher of music in an academy in a small provincial town in the Soviet Union, but because he was an intellect and spoke out against the Stalinist regime, he'd lost his job. After the war he'd managed to escape to Canada, to Toronto, where he was employed at Tip Top Tailors as an ironer. Someone had heard him sing at a Slavic reception and told him of the Doukhobor population in the west who were of Russian background and loved to sing. This was more than Mr. Ramirov had hoped for. A mother tongue and singing in common. He'd arrived in great expectation, by train two months ago, rented a small mushroom-coloured house in a back lane right behind Murphy's Drug Store, and proceeded to set up a music academy in his tiny living room.

So far we were his first students. Oh, he'd been hosted at several dinners and teas and listened attentively to the beautiful choir singing, even voiced his opinion in a mild way, but there was something about the tall, stoop-shouldered greying man with the intense eyes which precluded intimacy.

"Too quiet ... doesn't say much."

"How can he teach. He's an intellect, no fire."

The Annual Doukhobor Talent Show was coming up, and Zina and Marion and I decided we were going to sing. A trio. We'd never sung in public before, and Mr. Ramirov would show us. It would be a surprise. We'd pay in eggs and vegetables.

But we'd never expected such passion and emotion in so quiet a man.

Now we stared as he stood in front of us, waving the songbook, transformed.

"'Katoosha', a romance." He closed his eyes, began

to sing in a fine tenor. Of blossoming orchards, mists along the river and the young Katoosha walking along its banks, singing of her lover.

He had fled the tiny room, the trio of gawky schoolgirls, back to his land of balalaikas and cossacks. Until Zina's giggle broke the spell and he opened his eyes. A flash of anger, quickly replaced by a smile.

"Now you try. Zina, bass. Marion, you the soprano. You have the highest notes. And you, Ana." For a second he looked uncertain. "I suppose all that's left is the middle part. Not loud but with enthusiasm. Poitah." Sing.

He started off the first verse. We struggled along valiantly. He closed his eyes as if in pain at our flat notes, and continued singing.

"Now just you three." He waved his hand and we watched it, mesmerized. "Louder. Open your mouths. Let me hear each word." He took Marion's part, skimming over the high notes effortlessly. "More practice. Much much more practice. And please, sing with passion. Release your voices."

All afternoon Andrei Ramirov tried to create a trio of nightingales out of three giggling girls.

"Breath control. Hold the notes longer. Breathe from the diaphragm, not gasping like you're in pain. When you stop all together, I think maybe you don't start up again."

And finally, when we were hoarse and exhausted, "We'll stop for chai, young ladies," he said, and left the small stuffy room.

We looked around at the worn furniture, the two pictures on the wall. One, a sepia photograph of a young woman with a pale complexion, hair upswept, dark soulful eyes and beautifully molded mouth. The lace at her throat was secured by an exquisite brooch. The other picture was not as interesting, a small painting of a modest country home. Not the peasant kind we'd seen in our readers at Russian School, but the kind a poor aristocrat would live in. The house was set against a wood of white birch and tall evergreens and I could almost hear the wind sighing, see the trembling birch leaves.

Mr. Ramirov emerged from the kitchen, tea tray in hand. "Ah, you are looking at my painting. It was my home. Are the woods not magnificent." It was a statement.

I thought the woods in our valley were even more beautiful, but did not venture an opinion.

Tea in glasses, an old Russian custom, and lumps of sugar to hold in one's mouth and sip through. We sat on the edge of the dilapidated sofa and tried to act graceful, while holding onto the hot glasses.

"Who is the pretty lady?" I asked, more to initiate conversation than out of curiosity.

The eyes became hooded, the face impassive. After a long silence, during which I wished I'd never asked, he said in a colourless voice.

"Moya Zshenah." My wife.

Marion, who was remarkably unperceptive, said, "Oh, she's so pretty. What's her name?" in her most giggly schoolgirl voice.

"Sonya."

"Is she still in Toronto? Is she going to come here, too, or did she stay in Russia?" Marion was undaunted.

"Nyet."

"Nyet, she's not coming or nyet, she is still in Russia?"

"It's not Russia anymore. It is now Sovetskoi Soyooz.

Don't your parents teach you girls anything? Your grandparents once lived there. Didn't they tell you anything?"

"Of course they did. They taught us that the Russian military were mean to them and they had to leave because they were pacifist. We know all about that." Marian was angry.

Mr. Ramirov stood up. "One more time before you leave, young ladies." When the last hoarse note had died away, he said, "Practice, at least one hour each day. I shall see you next Sunday." He bowed formally and not knowing what else to do, we paused then solemnly bowed back.

We walked home in the darkening spring evening with the smell of old snow and warm rain and suppers being cooked behind the lamplit windows we passed, and the thought of Mr. Ramirov eating a lonely meal at home with his lovely Sonya far away somehow made me feel sad.

"I'll ask him to supper," I said, "Maybe we can find out about his wife."

"Maybe you should mind your own business, Ana," said Marion. She was still irritated with Mr. Ramirov. "Besides, the singing is supposed to be a surprise."

"I'll ask him not to say anything. He'll like mama's borsch. I'm sure his isn't as good."

"Of course not. Men can't cook."

"Andrei Ramirov for supper?" mama was surprised. "But why? And how do you know him?"

"I've said hello to him on the street," I said, crossing my fingers behind my back. "Besides, he looks lonely. And awfully thin. Don't you think he's thin?"

"Well, yes."

"And you know how good your borsch is. Besides

we might learn some Russian culture. You're always saying we don't speak enough Russian."

"All right, ask him for next Saturday evening. He looks like he could use a good meal. But I don't know what to talk to him about. I heard he hasn't got much to say."

"Papa will talk to him about singing or maybe ask about his family."

Monday after school, I walked downtown, through the shabby back alley behind Murphy's Drugstore, with its tumbled fences and candy wrappers in the dirty snow and soggy grey clothes on sagging clotheslines, to the small house in the lane.

Mr. Ramirov answered my timid knock. He was formally dressed as usual, white shirt, necktie. Papa always wore work clothes except for sobranye and choir practice.

"Please, come for supper this Saturday evening. Mama said to ask. We live way out at the end of Sand Creek Road, the very last house."

"Thank you." Surprised eyes widened.

"And please, don't say anything, you know, about the singing. It's supposed to be a secret."

All day Saturday I helped my mother make borsch, watched her pull out round golden loaves of bread from the old woodstove oven, and finally create her lemon meringue pie, served only to very special guests.

"The good wedding dishes, Ana," she said, and I knew this was no ordinary guest. "An aristocrat, used to the best, not of peasant stock like us." I felt guilty for putting her through all the work.

The knock on the door came precisely at five o'clock. Mama rushed to answer it, pulling off her apron, shoving it at me as she went by. She ushered in the elderly man, taking his umbrella and hat and faded silk scarf.

"Come in, come in, Mr. Ramirov. Glad you're here. My husband, you know him from the big choir — he's milking the cow. He'll be right in."

I cringed. Why did she have to mention the cow. I was sure Mr. Ramirov had never milked in his whole life.

"Sadees, sit, on the chesterfield. Ana will entertain you."

"And how is practise?"

"Fine. We sing every day after school." I didn't add that we were sick of Katoosha and her eternal walks along the misty river.

"Andrei, dobrai vecher," papa came into the room. He'd changed his milking clothes, but a faint odour of the barn hung in the air.

There was a clamour in the kitchen, recriminations, and then a crash. Embarrassed, I studied the worn linoleum I'd polished just that day with Johnson's Hard Wax. The Ramirov family undoubtedly had had a faithful servant to do menial tasks while the family sang, painted beautiful pictures and sipped tea in the cherry orchards.

We sat around the kitchen table with its oilcloth, under the umbrella of yellow light cast by the coal-oil lamp. Mama ladled steaming bowls of borsch, passed around bread, pie and tea. Did the Ramirovs dine on caviar in their country mansion among the birches?

"Your hymns are beautiful, but very sad," our guest stated as he sipped his chai.

"We've suffered hardships," papa said, "at the hands of the Tsars and the army. Tortured for our beliefs. My great-grandfather was sent to Siberia and never saw his family again. He died of hunger and the cold. Our people were moved around at the whim of the government. It seemed no one wanted a group of people who wouldn't fight for the Tsar and would rather go to prison than to war. And then this country took us in. Yes, our songs are sad."

"We too had our turn. My family," he stopped, looked down at his hands growing out of the frayed cuffs.

"What about your family? Where are they?" I said.

"Neemah." Gone.

"Gone where? What happened to them?" I ignored mama's frown.

The stove crackled. And somewhere in the night a coyote laughed.

"Are they in Toronto?" I ploughed on. "Will they be here soon?"

"Ana. You ask too many questions," papa said. "Please excuse her Andrei. She is very curious, and rude."

"The hour grows late and I have students tomorrow. They are proving a great challenge. I need my wits."

"I'll drive you home, and tell you about the song we're learning. It's by the Don Cossacks. I ordered the record all the way from Toronto. It took a whole month."

"Och Ana," mama said as we washed dishes. "Sometimes you open your mouth so wide when it should be closed so tight."

Next afternoon as we picked our way through the grimy snow, I hung back, wondering if Mr. Ramirov was upset with me. Papa hadn't said anything upon his return except "I think Andrei has sadness in his past" and "He'll be helping us with the new folk songs. He's not too good with the hymns."

Zina, unscathed by Mr. Ramirov's disapproval,

marched up the sagging steps and knocked loudly on the peeling door.

"Dobrai dyen, devooshkee." The face was polite, but closed. "Let me take your coats. Stand here. We will start the song. Open your mouths wide. Let the sound out. Breathe."

As we struggled through the song, I looked for the brooding eyes of Sonya. The picture was gone. Only the house in the wood remained, hanging on the dingy wallpaper. I saw Marion staring at the empty wall. Zina sang on, eyes wide on Mr. Ramirov's hands as he led us.

"Mr. Ramirov," said Marion carefully balancing her glass of chai, "Where is the picture of the beautiful lady ... your wife?"

I took a huge swallow, burnt my tongue, shocked by Marion's boldness. There was a long silence and then Mr. Ramirov, his face very red, said "You ask and ask about my family, my wife. Well ... I will tell you. My wife, Sonya, is a Jew. You know what that means? Have you heard of Stalin's bloody purges? Carried out in secret after the war? They took my wife. She's still there. Our two sons were killed in the war during the bombing. One day we were a family living in the country, the boys at school, I was teaching music. Then they were dead. A bomb struck the school. All our relatives were gone. There were just the two of us and for a time we wanted to die. But we struggled on through the war, and then afterwards the police controlled everything. Everyone hated the Jews and I being married to one was equally despised. We made plans to escape. Made our way to the station to take the train through Siberia and on to China. We chose a moonless night. Under cover of darkness we thought we would be safe. We carried no belongings, only pictures. Then they stopped the train, walked through the cars. We looked straight ahead, pretended we weren't afraid. But they smelled the fear, saw our eyes, apprehended us."

The voice was low, strained. We could hardly hear. I was wishing we hadn't asked, wishing he'd stop. "They didn't even look at our papers. They knew. They let me go and took her, wouldn't let us say goodbye. Just grabbed her. She had nothing with her except the pictures of the boys. I can still hear her screams as she was dragged off. I tried to go with her. They wouldn't let me, made me stay on the train. So I continued my journey. I was in a daze. I didn't know what else to do. I made my way to China then Europe and ended up in Toronto."

No one said anything. Finally he remembered us. "I've been trying to bring her to freedom through the embassy in Ottawa. Maybe someday I will, maybe. If she's still alive."

Two weeks later we walked onto the floodlit stage of the cultural centre, looked out at the vast audience in the semi-darkness. This was it. The weeks of practice, endless glasses of chai, curiosity, then pity for our instructor.

Earlier, we'd listened to the choirs, watched a skit, heard an impressive solo sung by a boy we all had a crush on, and listened sympathetically as the Salikin sisters sang an off-key duet.

Backstage we'd straightened our shawls, twitched our skirts in place, checked unfamiliar nylon seams.

"What if we're flat? My father would just die."

"So would Mr. Ramirov."

"Remember Ana, not too loud."

A numbness set in as we stared at the blur of expectant faces and waited for the murmurs to die down. In a daze I heard Zina sing the first line in a slightly shaky voice, heard Marion and I automatically join in. I was outside the window looking in, at the stage, at myself. I heard myself sounding the words, singing the tune, saw my tight white smile. I saw Mr. Ramirov in the front row. He looked excited, nodding and moving his hands slightly, directing us from his seat. And I wasn't afraid anymore. We had to sound good so Mr. Ramirov could get lots of jobs and bring his Sonya to Canada. And then it was over and the audience was nodding and applauding and in the front row Mr. Ramirov was smiling.

It was a week later, when a late winter storm left the world a cotton-batten fairyland, sounds muffled except for surprised spring birds. We were at Murphy's Drugstore looking at magazines, trying on cologne, when Mr. Ramirov walked in. He caught sight of us and came over, being careful on the muddy wooden floor.

"Devooshkee, I have great news." Blue eyes glowed fire. "My wife, Sonya, she has been found."

"Where? Where is she?" Marion said.

"Will you be going to her?" I said.

"She is in Montreal on her way here. The Russian Embassy in Ottawa has contacted me by telegram two days ago. The Soviet authorities allowed her to leave."

"When will she be here?" Zina said.

"Monday of next week. Arriving by train. I have much to do. I must get everything ready."

We stared at the departing figure, tall and spare in his old black coat, at the long straggly hair. In his excitement he'd forgotten his hat.

"I know, let's welcome Sonya too," I said.

"Maybe get some flowers," said Marion.

"Or bake a cake," I said.

"She'll like that," said Zina, "She'll be hungry when she comes. It's a long journey from Montreal."

"We'll make a sign in Russian. She might not read English."

We made plans, told our parents, even went to Fanny's Florals and asked if we could have some flowers at a discount.

Monday finally arrived. We were at the station early, but already a small cluster of curious onlookers were grouped on the platform. A stranger from overseas was a rare occurrence in our town.

Would she be wearing lace like in the picture, with her dark hair pinned up? Would she smile at her husband or would her eyes look sad? Would she throw her arms around him, or wait until he hugged her?

We could barely stand the excitement, shifting from one foot to the other, chattering, saying nothing, scanning the track, holding our sign and gifts.

"Dobro ootro, devooshkee," Andrei Ramirov strode unto the platform, smiling, his hair trimmed, carrying a small bouquet of white violets.

"The train is on time today. You must all come for chai soon, meet my Sonya properly. Sing 'Katoosha' for her. Wait, I hear it."

We saw the smoke, heard the roar, and watched the black engine puff into sight. Brakes squealed. Hissing steam covered the crowd on the platform.

The conductor jumped off and pulled down the steps. He began helping passengers down. We moved closer. Was it that woman? No. She had three small children. Or that enormous woman in the fur coat? No. Sonja would be romantic and thin and haunted-looking after her ordeal.

We waited.

Maybe she needed help getting off, or even had to be carried off.

Mr. Ramirov looked anxious, standing in front of the open doorway trying to see inside the passenger car, searching the windows.

"Is that her?" I saw a white face in the window.

"That's a man, silly."

The whistle startled us. Steps were pulled up and doors banged shut. We stared in bewilderment as the train pulled out, gathered speed and disappeared. The cluster of people dispersed, looking back at Mr. Ramirov as they left. Only dirty steam and a fading whistle remained as we stood, stunned, on the nearly empty platform.

We didn't look at Mr. Ramirov, until we were turning the corner that is, and I sneaked a look over my shoulder and wished I hadn't. He stood perfectly still, holding the little bouquet, tears streaming down his cheeks.

"Maybe she missed the train."

"Yeah. She'll come tomorrow. Let's leave these things at his house."

"Wait," I said. "Let's go to the Stargate for a Crush first. Until he gets home."

Later, we walked through the dirty, muddy lane and up his sagging steps.

Mr. Ramirov held the door open, "I must go next door to the pharmacy to place a telephone call to the embassy. Perhaps I got the day wrong. But the telegram did say 'Monday'." He looked at the crumpled yellow paper on the table.

"Here." We held out our offerings shyly. "Perhaps you can give them to her when she comes."

"Spaseebah." Thank you. "She will be pleased with your kindness." He left the room with the cake.

Sonya's picture once again hung on the wall and for

a moment we were silent, studying the brooding dark eyes. Then I moved toward the little table and picked up the telegram, straightened it and read aloud softly.

"To Andrei Ramirov from M. Snegov, Russian Embassy, Ottawa. STOP. As stated many times, our sources have verified your wife Sonya Ivanovna died in an accident soon after she was released from questioning. STOP. Again our condolences. STOP. Consider case closed. STOP.

Wings

The train station was crowded on the hot June afternoon that Henry Blackstone's body was shipped home. Almost the entire population of the valley was there to meet one of their boys. Henry's family, friends, his teachers and curious onlookers like us jammed the wooden platform and spilled over onto the cinder paths.

I could see Henry's parents, his mother's blonde hair carefully permed as usual, and his sisters walk through the crowd and enter the station house.

Henry had been in the Royal Canadian Air Force, stationed in Trenton, Ontario and his plane had crashed while on a training flight.

Henry had been at least three grades ahead of me, a tall thin boy with a dirty blonde crewcut and curious greyish freckles. I'd mostly remembered him playing basketball on the second-string in his white and green singlet, his scrawny body glistening with sweat. He seldom scored.

I had decided to get a summer job because I had my eye on a royal blue bomber jacket with grey collar in Eaton's catalogue. Everyone was buying bomber jackets that year, so I'd gone to Henry's father's farm with my friends Zina and Marion and we were hired to weed onions — acres and acres of bright green shoots stretching across fertile black loam, thickly surrounded by stubborn crab grass, dandelion and pigweed. There were at least ten of us in the work crew. The married women working quickly and chattering about kids, complaining about husbands. And us girls, dawdling well behind as we talked of clothes, boys and school and did you hear Pauline Woznoski was pregnant and wouldn't or couldn't say who the father was. We all believed the latter. And did you see the cute bathing suit in the co-op window, a two-piece number, my father would kill me.

Henry Blackstone came across the fields in the half-ton truck with "Blackstone Acres" painted on its blue sides. He sharpened our hoes as we self-consciously poked each other and tried to act grown-up. I caught him looking at me and I straightened the bandana over my hair, wishing I were wearing lipstick.

"Want a ride home?" he'd said to me and, a few minutes later, we were all in the back of the truck, giggling and swinging our dusty feet as we sat on the tailgate. Then Zina began singing a folk song in Russian and we joined in as loud as we could, looking over our shoulders to see if Henry could hear. I guess we were trying to embarrass him. Anglo-Saxon boys were seldom seen in the company of Doukhobor girls. They usually took out the girls who lived in the big houses downtown, to Friday night movies at the Regal, then to the Tally-Ho for a milkshake. My friends and I hung out at the Stargate Café, a Chinese greasy spoon where we sipped pop and fed the jukebox.

"My father would take the switch to me if I ever went out with an Angleek," Zina would say, but she'd toss her head and smile at them anyway.

Angleek was what we called anyone who wasn't Russian or Slovak or Japanese.

Henry let my friends off first and I was left alone in the back of the swaying old truck, dust streaming after us. We screeched to a stop and I jumped off, holding my hoe.

"Ana," Henry leaned out and I noticed the pimples on his nose. "I heard your friends call you that. Would you like to go for a ride tonight? I can take my father's Oldsmobile. Maybe we'll take in the show at the Regal."

I looked down at my dirt-caked shoes. "I can't. Not til I'm sixteen. And besides, you're not Russian." I ran toward the house where my sisters stared out the windows and the smell of fresh-baked bread greeted me.

"Mama, are we prejudiced?" I asked later, as I sat on the back steps reading the funnies in the *Free Press Weekly,* which arrived all the way from Winnipeg and took at least a week or more to get here.

"Why?"

"Well, I think that's what I heard Henry Blackstone call after me. He wanted to take me to the Regal tonight."

"You're far too young. Besides, he's not our kind."

"What is our kind? What's the difference, anyway?"

"We just fit in better with our own. It's easier because we understand each other's ways."

The cow in the cool field next to the garden made a low mooing sound as she settled in for the night.

"You know how some of those Angleekee look down on us," my mother continued. "Especially Mrs. Blackstone. You'd think she owns the whole town just because her grandfather was the first mayor."

"Zina says it's because they think we all burn and

bomb and strip."

"They know better. You have to learn to ignore them," she shrugged. "No use you getting your zlo up."

I didn't tell my mother about the big fight in the schoolyard last month, when that mouthy Herby Moore had decided to pick on Marion. She was his victim that week and every day he teased her at recess.

"When are you going to bomb the school, Douk?"

"Hey Marion, got a match?"

By Friday, Marion had had enough. She went after Herby, grabbing his hair, kicking at his groin, gouging his cheek with her nails.

Herby was taken by surprise, never expecting a girl, especially a Doukhobor girl who wasn't supposed to fight, to attack him like a grizzly.

The fight was over in seconds. Marion stood back panting, staring at Herby who was bent over, cheek bleeding.

Later in the washroom, Marion calmly rinsed Herby's blood off her hands as several girls stared at her in awe.

As we walked into the classroom, she whispered to me, "I hope my father and mother never find out, so don't you tell anyone, Ana."

My mother flipped to the Home Loving Hearts page. "Oh, here's a recipe for Sunshine Pickles for your hope chest scrapbook."

I rolled my eyes, kept on reading "Little Orphan Annie." I wasn't allowed to date, yet I was expected to work on my hope chest.

After that, Henry ignored me and my friends and one of the field hands drove us home.

That autumn Henry joined the Royal Canadian Air Force and came home in his uniform and suddenly was popular. We'd never known a pilot before, or seen a real plane for that matter, except to watch a dot moving across the sky. The only plane I'd seen up close was when a small plane had crashed into a field, killing the pilot, and which had reeked nauseatingly of spilled oil and scorched metal, and the whole town had trekked across the field to see the disaster. But now here was somebody who actually flew an airplane, or was going to as soon as he learned how.

I was wearing my new blue bomber jacket the day I walked downtown after school. The air was biting cold, dry brown leaves blowing around the frosty, rutted road, the thin ice crunching under my rubber boots. I shifted *The History of the Ancient and Medieval World* to my left arm and shivered in the wind. I'd taken a different route that day, a shortcut down a sidestreet, past the big houses where the trees clacked their bare branches against second and third story windows.

Suddenly I sprawled on the icy walk, books scattered, red plaid skirt above my knees, the world upside down. I scrambled up, then sat down quickly as pain stung my knee. A stickiness oozed through my torn stocking. I looked around, feeling foolish, but could see no one.

The stained glass door of the white house directly across the street opened and Henry Blackstone emerged. He quickly walked across the white-pillared veranda and ran down the steps toward me. I don't think he knew who it was until he stood over me.

"Oh. It's you. Are you hurt? Your knee's bleeding." He was squinting, neither friendly nor unfriendly. A thin, gangly boy, with pale blue eyes, awkward and homely. And he wasn't even wearing his glamorous uniform.

Oh, why couldn't he be good looking, I thought as I

struggled to my feet. I was shy and a little repelled by him.

"Come in the house," he said. "And wash up your knee."

I hesitated.

"You can't walk home like that. Come in and clean up."

"I ... I don't know. My mother will be waiting for me."

"Well," he looked uncertain, "I think you should clean it up. I can drive you home afterwards."

A vision of me arriving home in a car with a young man danced before my eyes.

"Oh no," I gasped, "I can walk. Really. But if it's all right, I would like to wash my knee."

Normally, I'd be blushing and stammering in the presence of a male several years older than me, but I didn't consider Henry attractive.

We walked up the steps and into the house.

"Put your things here," he pointed to a table near the door. I dropped my books and looked around. Dark shiny furniture was grouped on glowing Oriental rugs. I'd seen them in magazines. We had shiny linoleum at home and lots of homemade rag rugs. Here were vases and shelves of books and, in the corner, a large piano. So this was how the rich people lived. I limped over to the piano, put out a hand and touched the keys.

"We'd better go up to the bathroom and you can wash off all that blood."

I took off my bomber jacket and draped it over a green silk chair with brocade flowers.

I followed Henry up the wide curving staircase, my hand sliding up the smooth bannister. We passed large bedrooms and I glimpsed satin bedspreads and matching curtains and thought of my worn yellow chenille spread.

Henry stopped and pushed open a door at the end of the hall.

"You can wash up here," he said, handing me a cloth, "and you can put on some ointment and a bandage." He put everything on the counter and left. I was glad he hadn't offered to help.

As I washed grit out of the cut, I looked around. Imagine — a toilet right in the house. We had an outhouse back of the gooseberry bushes, and chamberpots in winter. Mirrors lined the entire room and I thought of our one wavy mirror, usually with several faces looking in it at the same time. But it was the bathtub that made me catch my breath. Big and deep and luxurious, and I imagined myself slipping into hot scented bubbly water instead of the six inches of tepid water in the tin tub which we dragged into the kitchen on Friday nights.

I spread ointment on my knee. We used plain Iodine with its skull and crossbones label and terrible sting. After I'd attached the large bandage and taped it on, I limped out into the hall and took a backward look, memorising each exquisite detail.

I turned to go down the hall and found myself face to face with Mrs. Blackstone. I recognized her immediately as the sophisticated woman in pretty dresses and matching hats who shopped only at Sylvia's Style Centre and City Grocery. Never the co-op Store like us.

But I hardly knew this Mrs. Blackstone. Her neat waves tumbled over her shoulders and she wore a dressing gown. We never wore dressing gowns during the day unless we were sick. But this wasn't like my mother's blue housecoat with buttons up to the chin.

Mrs. Blackstone's robe was a gauzy pink and gaped open down to her bosom, and was held together in the middle with a thin sash. I was so embarrassed, I just stood in the doorway, tongue-tied.

"Who the hell are you?" the voice sounded blurred. I saw a glass half-full of golden liquid and it dawned on me that Mrs. Blackstone was drunk.

"I was just going."

"How did you get in? Did you break in? I'm calling the police." And she turned quickly, almost tripping over her long hem.

"Henry let me in."

She stopped, teetered and turned, her face red. "Henry? You mean my fool of a son has a girl and has even sneaked her upstairs?"

"No. It's not like that. I fell and hurt my knee."

She laughed and almost lost her balance, then grabbed at the railing. I looked down into Henry's horrified face as he made his way up the stairs.

"Aren't you one of those Doukhobor girls?" She emphasised "those" like I was a harlot or something. "No wonder Henry's sneaking around. He knows his father would disown him, so don't you get any ideas."

"I don't want to go out with him," I shouted. "And I'm not his girl. My father would kill me if I ever went out with him." I rushed down the stairs, brushing past Henry.

"Ana, wait," Henry ran after me, grabbing up my coat, as if the action would keep me from leaving. "I didn't know she was home. Don't tell anyone about her. Please." He sounded desperate.

"You mean that she's a drunk?" I said nastily. She'd smelled just like old Jim, our neighbour down the road, when he visited us on a Saturday night.

"Yeah, but don't tell anyone, please," Henry whispered. "No one knows except my family and our best friends. That's why I left home. I couldn't stand it anymore. The fights, being scared someone would find out, trying to keep her indoors and hiding the car keys. Our family built this town, you know. They're written up in the history of the valley over at the museum and everything. And my great-grandfather's picture is in city hall."

"I won't tell," I said, ashamed for him, wanting to escape. "Don't worry, I won't."

"Here," Henry went to the closet and removed his air force jacket. He fumbled with a pin and held it out to me. I looked at his outstretched palm where the light caught the gold of his air force wings.

"I can't."

"Yes. Take it. Just promise not to say anything."

He put the pin in my hand and closed my fingers over it.

"I promise." I picked up my coat and books and ran out the door and down the steps into the blue twilight of the winter afternoon. I didn't stop running until I was a block away, when I became conscious of the pain in my knee.

I avoided Henry after that and he must have been avoiding me because I didn't see him before he went back to Ontario. I kept the wings in the bottom of my little red jewellery box, underneath my locket and the imitation pearl necklace from page 281 of Eaton's catalogue.

Sometimes I toyed with the idea of wearing the wings to school pinned to my new pale green Dalkieth sweater, but I knew it would cause so much talk, my mother would hear immediately from my girlfriends' mothers. It would be a bigger scandal than the time Rosie Jablonsky had a shotgun wedding at fifteen.

So I'd look at the pin when I was alone and when I met Mrs. Blackstone, I'd look away, and she'd stare at me as if I were a fly she'd found in her soup.

It was late spring and the air was filled with lilacs and roses and the windows of the high school were open to catch the warm breezes. Notes were passed around and whispers punctuated the stale air as Mr. Stevens droned on about fractions.

Suddenly the public address system crackled and we looked up expectantly at the box high above the blackboard, glad of the diversion.

"Your attention please," the principal's authoritative voice filled the room. "I am sorry to announce that one of our former students, Henry Blackstone, was killed in a training flight in Ontario yesterday. His body will arrive at the train station the day after tomorrow. You may wish to be there as an expression of your sympathy to the Blackstone family. Thank you."

The p.a. clicked off and Marion and Zina and I stared at each other, stunned. Not a sound was heard, except old Mr. Lawrence's lawnmower outside the window. Mr. Stevens finally cleared his throat.

"All right, class, let's continue. What's the common denominator here?"

No one paid attention. Cara Flynn, Henry's next door neighbor, was crying and everyone was whispering, then talking loudly.

"Class! Pay attention." Mr. Stevens' face was scarlet. "I said 'what's the common denominator?' And anyone else who talks will get detention."

On Saturday afternoon, my girlfriends and I hurried downtown to the train station. It seemed like everyone was there that hot day. We crowded onto the cinder paths and looked anxiously down the track. Henry's family arrived in their maroon Oldsmobile and climbed up the steps to the wooden platform where the crowd made a path for them. They looked neither left nor right as they walked into the station. We heard the shrill of the train whistle, followed by a rumble and the train steamed into view, brakes squealing. It ground to a painful stop and black soot and steam billowed out over the crowd.

The conductor jumped off and a few passengers alighted. People began unloading freight. The doors of one of the baggage cars was thrown open and it was here that our eyes were riveted. A long, narrow wooden box was handed out and carefully placed on a station trolley.

"That's Henry," Zina said excitedly. "Oh God ... I can't believe he's in there. Can you?"

I didn't answer, just stared in fascination at the box being trundled down the platform. Some of our women teachers were crying and so were many other women, mostly mothers and young girls. Henry had never been a basketball star, or good-looking or popular. But today, he was a hero.

The Blackstones walked out of the station house and followed their dead son down the steps, as he was put in the hearse, then got in their car and drove off.

The crowd on the platform became noisy as people once again went about their business.

"They're having a private funeral," Marion said. "I saw where his grave's dug in the English cemetery."

I didn't know whether to say anything about the wings or not. Henry was gone and I didn't like his mother, so it would serve her right if everyone knew she was a drunk. I thought of my promise and kept silent.

The following day Henry was buried and when no one was looking, my friends and I added white lilacs from our gardens to the beautiful sprays on the earthen mound. I thought about coming back alone some time and leaving the wings on the grave.

I met up with Mrs. Blackstone on the street and she pretended not to know me, but in the instant before she looked away, I saw a flicker of something in her eyes and I knew she disliked me because I'd stumbled on her secret.

I wanted to tell someone. My mother, who'd say I shouldn't have been at the Blackstones in the first place. Or Zina and Marion, but they'd either tell everyone or wouldn't believe me. I carried the pin in my red plastic purse, knotted up in a corner of my cotton hanky. Maybe one day I'd show it to my friends. It was exciting to have a big secret. If only Henry had been handsome and I'd had a crush on him and he'd given me the wings because he liked me, it would be so romantic and sad. This way, it was just a bribe, even though he'd asked me out once, a long time ago.

My friends and I were in the Tally-Ho Ice Cream Parlour and Coffee House one rainy Saturday morning. It was autumn, damp and windy, with wet leaves covering the sidewalks. The Tally-Ho was cosy and warm and coffee-scented against the greyness outside, with beautiful old plates on the walls, an ancient, silver cash register, and carved dark wooden booths. We were in a booth near the back, sipping coffee, which I wasn't allowed until I was older, "stunts your growth," and which I ordered whenever I had the chance. I was taller than all the boys in class and a little worried I wouldn't stop growing.

The door opened and Mrs. Blackstone swept in,

followed by two of her friends. They shook their umbrellas and brushed raindrops off their smart raincoats, then sat down in the next booth and ordered coffee, paying no attention to us.

And then I heard the cool, cultured voice say clearly, "I don't know what's happening to this town. Grandfather Davidson would turn over in his grave if he saw all the riff-raff in his favourite coffeehouse."

There were murmurs of agreement and, before I knew it, I was fumbling furiously in my purse.

"What's the matter, Ana?" Zina said. "You look funny."

All the months of keeping quiet about the wings and about Mrs. Blackstone's secret all came to a head and bubbled over like a poison and I hardly realized what I was doing.

I found the handkerchief containing the wings in the bottom of my purse, untied it, and walked over to the next booth.

"I think you should have these, Mrs. Blackstone. Henry gave them to me, but I never really wanted them."

I laid the wings carefully on the table in front of her, then quickly walked out of the Tally-Ho.

Gabriel and the Salesman

When a cloud of dust heralded the approach of a car, we came running. Everyone we knew drove a horse and buggy or a pickup truck. And then, when the visitor turned out to be a travelling salesman, our excitement knew no bounds. It might be the Watkins man, with his wonderful array of bottles containing delicious nectars, cans of pie fillings and spices. Or the Raleigh salesman, selling ointments to heal cuts on the farm animals, cold remedies like chest rubs and syrups, and sweet smelling pomades for our hair.

This particular summer afternoon I was visiting baba on the farm when I saw the big, shiny convertible with its top down coming up the dusty drive, right through the cow pies and thistles. We didn't get many visitors on these winding mountain roads, so I dropped my hoe, jumped over the rows of wax beans and raced toward the car. A heavy middle-aged man with greased-back hair was pulling a case from a Meteor. I noted his white shirt which stuck wetly to his body, and white shoes, and figured he must be very rich. Papa wore a white shirt only on Sundays and this was Tuesday. And I'd never seen white shoes on a man before. He turned toward me and smiled with large white teeth.

"Hello, little girl," he winked at me, and I decided he was a wolf. "Slivka's the name, but you call me Al. Is your mama home?"

"It's my babushka, and she's in the house."

"Righto, little lady," he said and followed me inside, where baba was baking bread.

"What you sell today?"

She led the way into the livingroom where Mr. Slivka opened his case and spread out cloths on the doily-covered sofa. There were wonderful silks, shiny satins, sturdy rayons and taffetas in watery designs. A jumble of delicate laces, wide bands in snowy white and narrow ones in ecru, and a glorious array of ribbons.

Baba reached out and stroked a length of yellow taffeta, her work-roughened fingers making a raspy sound on the smooth cloth.

"Kraseevaya," she said. So pretty.

"And what a beautiful zanaveska it would make for sobranye," said Mr. Slivka.

Baba especially liked to dress up for sobranye, the meeting she attended each Sunday, and she already had several zanaveskas, the dainty aprons the women wore over their Sunday best. They were her one weakness and she had a zanaveska to match every outfit and every occasion.

"It's the last length I have," said the salesman. "I got it on special order from my Italian supplier, and I sold it all in Penticton and Kelowna, so there's not another like it for a hundred miles. You'll be the finest lady at sobranye. You know, a couple of women in town wanted it, but I saved it for someone like you. What do you think? Do you like it?"

I saw the longing in baba's eyes. "It's very nice, and I have egg money." She stared hard at the cloth, hesitated, then, "I take it," and went into the kitchen for the money.

Mr. Slivka added a length of white lace, a yard of narrow green ribbon and some thread.

"That's three dollars even. And you'll have the finest zanaveska." He sniffed the air. "Something sure smells good."

"Sit down. Eat. I cook vegetable soup and pirahi today."

"Why thank you. I've already been invited for supper in town, but this looks so good, I think I'll eat here."

He sat down at the kitchen table and had three helpings of soup and two of pirahi.

"Baba, I don't think I like that Mr. Slivka very much," I said that evening as I watched her cut out her zanaveska.

"Why Ana, he seem like very nice man. And he sell me this beautiful material. I will be prettiest lady at sobranye."

"He smiles with his teeth," I said, "Not his eyes."

Each night that week, baba worked on her zanaveska, and Saturday night it was ready. Sunday morning saw us squeezed into the little buggy, heading toward town. Baba asked me to sit in the back, so we wouldn't crease her creation, and she kept smoothing it down and smiling as we bumped along. We were late in arriving and deda hurriedly tied up the horse and followed us into the large brick building where the first hymn was already in progress.

Baba and I adjusted our headshawls then walked inside and bowed low. Deda joined the men while grandma and I went over to the women's side and sat down. For the next two hours, as we sang and listened to speeches and psalms, baba kept looking around, trying to see if her friends were present. The last hymn was sung and we poured out into the sunshine and joined the groups of people catching up on the week's happenings.

"Tina, how are you?" Baba greeted her friend in Russian. They stood smiling at each other, baba waiting for her friend to admire her zanaveska.

Finally she said, "Noo, how you like my new zanaveska? Dog swallow your tongue?"

Then baba lowered her eyes and saw what I'd been staring at. For there, on Tina's well-rounded stomach, was displayed a yellow taffeta zanaveska with a purple ribbon, and a band of mauve lace.

"Where did you get it, Natasha?" Tina said slowly. "Salesman say there only one like it."

They looked around, and in the yard full of colourful Sunday outfits, no less than twelve yellow zanaveskas fluttered in the breeze. The other women were pointing at each other, smiling or scowling, depending on their disposition, and I observed little Mrs. Zibin unobtrusively take off her zanaveska and quickly fold it into a tiny square.

There was a long pause, then, "Well, Tina, I guess we fools."

Voices broke out.

"Bes sovistnai." He has no shame.

"Sabacheeyee glaza." Eyes of a dog.

"Brakhoochiye." Liar.

"Yaroondah." Good for nothing.

We were silent on the way home and when we returned, I was told to change my clothes and feed the chickens. I knew baba was terribly embarrassed. She was a strong woman, despite her diminutive size, and hated looking foolish. I poured fresh water for the chickens, then scattered grain on the hardpacked ground, all the while keeping a sharp eye out for Gabriel, baba's bad-tempered rooster. Baba called him zolota, her treasure, but I thought he belonged in someone's soup pot. I was often the object of his vicious attacks, and longed for the day he'd be sold. However, as long as he was in the pen, I was safe.

Summer passed and baba made me a yellow taffeta blouse for school, and it was well into autumn before we saw the salesman again. I was spending the weekend on the farm, helping baba make sauerkraut to store in the root cellar, when the cloud of dust appeared down our road. The blue convertible, top up this time, purred to a stop and Mr. Slivka once again pulled out his case and walked up the steps, whistling.

Baba answered his knock and asked him in, and I held my breath, waiting for the tirade. Boy, was he going to get it. However, she didn't say anything as he spread out his cloths. Any minute now she'd start yelling at him.

I slowly let out my breath because baba was murmuring quietly as she looked at the material, even fingering this ribbon, that lace.

Finally, in a quiet voice she said, "Docha, please talk to Mr. Slivka. I be back soon," and hurried from the room.

I didn't say anything, just watched Mr. Slivka's hands with the black hairs on the back shake out the cloths and drape them on the furniture. To my relief, baba soon returned.

"Look, auntie," he said, and she stiffened at the familiarity. I braced myself. This was it. I'd seen my deda leave for the barn after one of her tongue lashings. Still she kept quiet. I was beginning to think she was sick.

"You'd look very pretty in this flowered rayon, auntie. Just perfect for a winter blouse. Hong Kong Rose, it's called."

"No. I not buy today."

"Oh ... then how about this blue stripe. It would make a nice skirt."

"No. I not buy."

"Say, is that fresh borsch I smell? I can always tell when someone's cooking borsch from a mile down the road."

"I cook borsch today."

A long pause, then, "Well, I'll be going, I guess." And he began grabbing at the cloths and ribbons, stuffing them helter skelter into his case. His face was scarlet and he didn't say a word, just snapped the lock shut and strode out of the house, whistling tunelessly, a bit of Hong Kong Rose sticking out of the case. He slammed the door as he left.

"Baba ... you didn't say anything about the zanaveska. I thought you were mad."

"Shhh ..."

Baba watched the departing Mr. Slivka out the kitchen window. She was still, as if waiting for something to happen. She opened the window and we both put our heads outside, but I didn't know what we were waiting for.

Suddenly, a terrible yell pierced the air as Gabriel flew across the yard and attached himself firmly to Mr. Slivka's leg. He tried frantically to shake off the bird, beating at him and swearing. I could have told him to save his wrath. Gabriel would let go when he was ready and that was after he'd firmly sunk his sharp beak into one's anatomy. I also could have told him that only baba's sharp "eedee, teep teep," come here chickie, would make the nasty creature let go. But grandma wasn't saying anything, just watching.

Mr. Slivka reached the car and attempted to get in, kicking ineffectually at his tormentor. Baba went to the porch and called, "Gabriel ... teep teep teep," and the rooster let go and came running.

Mr. Slivka took the opportunity to jump in the car and soon the robin's-egg blue Meteor was attacking the road, dust billowing behind it.

"But how did Gabriel get out? He was in the pen. I saw him earlier."

Baba didn't answer. Just held her beloved pet and gently stroked his iridescent orange and green feathers.

"Good boy," she said. "Good boy."

Head Cook at Weddings and Funerals

"The most wonderful day in a mother's life is when her daughter marries into a good family," I often heard Aunt Florence say. "Because she knows her girl will be taken care of for the rest of her life."

My mother would agree with her sister, then look around at her three daughters with a somewhat worried expression.

Aunt Florence, predictably, had married well. Her husband's relatives were all pillars of the Doukhobor community, while my mother had married a man who, although devout and hardworking, had relatives on his mother's side who were not as desirable as those of Aunt Florence's in-laws. However, I enjoyed visiting my father's family in their small house with its faint aura of decadence much more than I did Aunt Florence's home in the Doukhobor village.

Aunt Florence and Uncle Fred had a son, Fred Junior, who'd married well to an agreeable and pretty girl named Tina, from an upstanding Doukhobor family. They proceeded to move into the apartment right across the courtyard from Fred's parents and produce little Fred, much to the delight of Aunt Florence.

Aunt Florence's other child was a girl, my cousin Marusa, four years older than I. Her mother had great expectations of Marusa, who was extraordinarily pretty with her dark curls, sparkling brown eyes and tiny figure. A figure much enhanced by the fitted gabardine skirts she wore, the delicate nylon blouses with little artificial bouquets of flowers at the throat, or the soft, fuzzy pastel sweaters. I felt awkward and plain next to her. I was a giraffe with straight blonde hair and pale blue eyes.

When I visited her house, Marusa could sometimes be pleasant, even fun. Not stuck-up like she was at school. She let me try on her earrings and makeup, but only if she was in the mood.

"She can have her pick of all the nicest Doukhobor boys," Aunt Florence would say. "You should see Saturday morning at our place. The fancy cars and pickup trucks come in a stream, asking Marusa to go to the movies that night. She'll marry well."

Marusa was almost seventeen by now and dating for nearly a year. Aunt Florence hoped to have her settled down before her nineteenth birthday. Marusa would be finished high school next spring and had already filled her soondook for she'd learned to knit at six, embroider at eight.

She was taking the General Program in high school — typing, shorthand and business math. No use studying university courses when your ambition was to be married soon. A girl could get a job in a local office until she married and began raising a family, usually within a year of the wedding.

Aunt Florence would visit our chaotic little house outside of town, listen to mama's pleas for us girls to help with the work, and say with a touch of smugness,

"My Marusa is so cheerful, she likes helping me."

However, I knew Marusa could be stubborn, even mean-tempered.

That winter, which was a cold one, my father decided I was old enough to go to Sunday night sobaranye with him, while my mother stayed home with Sara and Lisa.

One particularly frigid night, I was sitting at the back of the meeting hall near the airtight heater, sweaty in my long woollen coat, wiggling cold toes in the tight overshoes. The two pairs of socks hadn't helped.

I wasn't paying attention to the hymns or the speeches, which were especially lengthy tonight. Several men had attended an important sezd, a convention, in Saskatchewan and had much to report.

Instead, I was watching my cousin who was sitting on a wooden bench, third row second from the end on the women's side, making eyes at Peter Zarubin. She was looking remarkably pretty in an embroidered platok, headshawl, her eyes dancing as she smiled at Peter.

Peter was a tall, gawky young man with a too-short haircut and a pleasing personality. He wasn't very good-looking except when he smiled and showed his dimples. He was showing a lot of dimples tonight.

Peter was considered an exceedingly good catch, especially by the mothers of marriageable daughters. His parents had a small tidy farm, vast apple orchards, a large ranch house with many bedrooms to accommodate their four sons. Mable Zarubin, Peter's mother, was a hard-working opinionated woman who kept a clean home and was a renowned cook. In fact her borsch became so famous, she'd graduated to head cook at weddings and funerals.

Most of the women in the Doukhobor community

helped out with cooking at these important events. The huge wedding feast required several settings, depending on the number of friends and relatives invited, as did the after-funeral meal serving the singers, gravediggers and family of the deceased.

Always at these occasions, in the place of honour at the dining table, there was the borsch. The special soup, thick with vegetables, laced with rich cream. The dish every young girl learned to cook at her mother's side.

Peter's mother had impressed the older women with her knowledge as to the right amount of butter and whipping cream, the correct pinch of dill, the quick and pretty way she shredded the cabbage, diced potatoes. So it was at an early age that she became head cook, instructing the other cooks, tasting, giving the final nod to the borsch before it was carried out to the tables by the serving women.

After the sobranye that cold night, I followed my father to our pickup, waited while he started the motor, cleared frost off the windshield. I saw Peter follow Marusa outside, tug at the silken fringes of her shawl, watched her jerk away and toss her head. A Doukhobor courting ritual I'd seen many times.

Marusa and Peter began going steady that spring and the following Christmas she received an engagement ring with a tiny diamond.

"Waste of money," papa said. "Better to buy a new stove for their home."

"Marusa let me try it on." I'd waited until my father had gone outside before imparting this important news. "And it cost fifty-four ninety-five. Second most expensive in Eaton's catalogue."

"Page 70," said Sara. "Ordered from Toronto. Not Regina like our boots and underwear."

"A ring is hardly important to a marriage, but a good cook is," — my mother's voice was caustic, envious of Aunt Florence whose children had chosen well, while she still had three young daughters to marry off. She was chopping borsch cabbage, showing us how to cut the strands long and fine. "Mable will expect her daughter-in-law to help with the cooking at home. You know there's a house full of men there." But she sounded pleased instead of sympathetic with Marusa.

It was late spring and Aunt Florence and mama were stitching Marusa's wedding quilt in our living room, when Marusa said, "I want to wear a wedding gown." Just like that. As if she were announcing she was hungry and wanted a cheese sandwich.

It was so unexpected that for a minute we kept on doing what we had been doing. Needlework, reading, playing checkers. When the meaning had sunk in, we all stopped, looking not at Marusa but at Aunt Florence.

Aunt Florence took a big breath, her bosom getting large. She turned and looked at Marusa, then at mama, and let her breath out long and slow, making a funny wheezing noise like Uncle Fred's accordian when he closed it. "Well, you can't," she said in a mild way.

This time we all looked at Marusa. Her cheeks were red and she wore her stubborn look.

"Ever since I was very little I've wanted to wear a wedding gown and a veil when I got married, mama." The words came out precisely.

Aunt Florence put down her needle, got up from the floor, faced her daughter with an equally stubborn look.

"You'll wear a Doukhobor skirt and blouse as planned. As for the veil, I'm embroidering a new shawl."

"I picked out a wedding gown in Eaton's. Only sixty-nine dollars and it's got lace flounces."

"I've already ordered lace from the cloth salesman. We won't talk about it anymore."

"Rosie wore a gown."

"Rosie didn't marry a Doukhobor boy. You have to go with tradition. What would people say. And your mother-in-law head cook too. You'll ruin your marriage before it's even started."

Aunt Florence got down on her knees, began stitching, not looking at us.

Marusa, still redfaced, stared at her mother's ample back end, then walked out of the room, through the kitchen, slammed the door so that the ornaments on the wall rattled. Not at all like someone who'd just decided to agree with her mother.

Soon afterwards, Marusa graduated from high school and obtained a summer job at Fogle's Garage doing basic bookkeeping and answering the phone. I'd see her that summer around town, in her crisp cotton dresses, hair pulled back in a ponytail, tiptoeing around the grease in the garage, enjoying the admiring looks of the mechanics. Or sometimes on her lunch hour, she'd be at the co-op, in serious discussion with a clerk about tea towels and pillow cases. After work I'd see her riding with Peter on her way home, sitting so close "she's almost in his lap," "... but they're engaged," my friends said with envy.

On a hot evening, a few days after Marusa's eighteenth birthday, just as we were finishing supper dishes in the stifling kitchen, Peter's new pink and white Pontiac with the chrome fins drove into our yard. Peter had quit school and got on at the sawmill, making payments to the credit union on the car.

Through the screen door, we watched Marusa lift a big box from the back seat, give it to Peter and hand in hand they walked up the steps.

"Come in, come in both of you," mama bustled about, taking off her stained apron and shoving shoes into a corner. "Have you had your supper? It won't take me a minute to set the table, heat the soup. I made it with fresh peas from the garden."

I stared at mama. Now that Marusa was almost a wife, she'd suddenly acquired a dignified new status. Above waitress or store clerk or even secretary. Only a teacher or nurse were superior to a well-married woman.

"Thank you, tyota, but we've already eaten at Peter's place. His mother taught me to make galooptsi."

"Yours were even better than my mother's," Peter said.

Peter must be blind in love, I thought. Unless she'd improved vastly, Marusa was a careless cook. I'd seen her vareniki come apart in boiling water, fillings bubbling on top, pastry wrappers floating merrily.

"I want to show you something," Marusa said.

She untied string from the box, pushed aside tissue, lifted out lace and satin.

"Page 352, Eaton's catalogue," I breathed.

"Marusa, what have you done?" Mother's shocked voice.

"Isn't it beautiful? And look at the veil."

"But I saw your mother sewing your wedding clothes," mama said.

"She doesn't know. I borrowed the money from Peter."

"You should tell your mother right away. I don't think she'll let you wear it."

"It's my wedding and I should wear whatever I want. But I want you to tell her. She won't listen to me." Marusa had her stubborn look.

"Oh Marusa, you should wear it. It's just beautiful."

"Quiet, Ana, this is none of your business. Marusa," she turned to her niece, "You must tell your mother yourself."

"She's too worried about what Peter's mother will say." She looked at Peter, who was fidgeting with his car keys. "Well? Don't you think I should wear what I want for my own wedding?"

"Your mother and mine won't like it," he said in a mild, hesitant voice.

"Whose wedding is it anyway? I thought it was ours."

She scooped up the gown, stuffed it into the box and marched outdoors, ponytail bobbing. Peter followed, looking worried.

"Do you think they'll break up?" Lisa asked. "And what will happen to the wedding cake?"

"We'll eat it," said Sara practically.

"Maybe Marusa will be an old maid."

Two weeks before the wedding, the zapoy, engagement ceremony, was held at the home of the bride's parents and the betrothed couple was officially blessed by their families.

Marusa was a demure bride-to-be, virtuous and pale and virginal in her pink Doukhobor blouse and skirt, her fringed shawl. Eyes downcast, she and Peter knelt and bowed to their parents.

Nothing was said about the wedding gown since the visit to our place, and we assumed it had been returned to Eaton's unworn and that Marusa had decided to be pliant. We'd admired the wedding blouse and skirt Aunt Florence had created, with its white lace over satin, dozens of pearl buttons, and tiny nipped-in waist. Marusa would be a radiant bride.

It was a clear and dewy summer morning. A beautiful day to be married. We were up early, rushed through chores and breakfast, dressed in new clothes purchased at the co-op. Hurried to the bride's home to help with the cooking and the table setting.

Wonderful smells came from the vast kitchen. Huge loaves of bread and a dozen varieties of cakes and pies were sitting on the counter, waiting to be cut. The pirahi, light pastries filled with vegetables or cottage cheese then baked pale golden, were piled high in a pan, making my mouth water. Rice and raisin plov was being stirred on the stove, salads and trays of fruit were sliced, chopped, arranged, set out on the tables.

The centrepiece of the meal, the borsch, was being cooked that very minute to be served fresh and fragrant at the wedding feast. The woman in charge of the borsch was not as famous as Mable Zarubin, and Aunt Florence eyed the proceedings apprehensively during her frequent trips to the kitchen.

The entire village was a beehive. Cooks were chopping, tasting, "Will it be as good as Mable's borsch? We can't let our family down." Long tables were set in the living room. Pincurled cousins considered important questions — should the bride and groom eat borsch from the same bowl according to tradition, or be modern and use two bowls? And where should the ceremonial table with bread, salt and water be placed?

Finally, everyone ran outdoors as the streamered cars and pickup trucks honked into the yard. The big Zarubin family and their friends walked across the courtyard and up the steps of the verandah. We watched Peter, unfamiliar in his new suit, and his parents, approach the bride's family, Mable holding an enormous loaf of bread in front of her.

Formal greetings. Low bows.

"We've come for the bride."

"She's here," Uncle Fred said, "Come in." Aunt Florence stood beside him, holding her own large loaf of bread.

And from the back of the crowd ... Marusa walked out, head high, looking straight ahead, and stood beside her parents. She wore the wedding gown from Eaton's.

Looking back on that moment, I can remember the silence which followed Marusa's appearance. The almost-fainting look on Aunt Florence's face. Marusa's defiant look. I felt a numbness at the time, but thinking about it today, I can recall the divided thoughts I had as Marusa made her appearance — excitement because it was so totally unexpected, so deliciously sinfully disobedient, and the sinking feeling as I saw Mable Zarubin's shocked expression. Would she take her son, unmarried, and go home? The wedding day over before it had begun? Only Peter seemed oblivious, smiling at his bride, taking her hand.

Uncle Fred, his face red all the way up his bald forehead and into the hair combed carefully across the thinnest part, cleared his throat, said, "Let us start the prayers" in a funny strangled voice, clasped his hands over his plump stomach, closed his eyes and began to recite a psalm.

As the ceremony proceeded, I heard murmurs, "Ona yamoo pakazsha," she'll show him. "Ona krasaveetsa," too pretty. "She'll wear the pants in the family." "Mable will teach her what Florence didn't." "Maybe she'll have bebeechka next year and that'll settle her down."

After the psalms had been recited, the hymns sung, Aunt Florence unrolled the prayer rug which had been brought over all the way from Russia so long ago, and Marusa and Peter began the bowing. They knelt on their knees and bowed to their parents, to their grandparents, to every aunt and uncle and cousin, touching their foreheads to the ground, kissing everyone.

Marusa and Peter stood up and faced us and we all shouted "maladim dobrai chass" to the newlyweds, good luck.

The ceremony at the bride's home was over. It was time for feasting. From my place near the foot of the table I could see the enormous steaming bowl of borsch set down in front of Mable.

She ladled her borsch. Only one ladle? Did it look greasy? Perhaps not the right shade of orange? Too many tomatoes ... the cabbage coarse ... too much dill? Mama and Aunt Florence looked at each other.

Then everyone turned and looked at Mable. Mable buttered a slice of bread, looked down at her bowl with a slight frown. She held the fringes of her shawl to one side as she bent her head over the bowl, lifted the spoon with borsch in it, put it into her mouth, withdrew it, chewed the contents, a thoughtful look on her face.

Mable Zarubin, head cook at weddings and funerals, swallowed, looked unsmilingly across the table at Aunt Florence, solemnly said, "it is good ... very good," and, still holding the fringes aside, began eating her borsch, stopping now and then for a bite of bread. She refilled her bowl, smacked her lips and continued eating. Aunt Florence took a big breath and beamed.

After the meal I helped clear the table, mindful of my new wedgies and striped taffeta dress with the big crinoline.

Mable and her sister Doonya came into the kitchen, loaded with dirty dishes.

"It was good borsch, very good. But two bowls? I tell you, Doonya, it's hard being head cook," Mable sounded satisfied. "But what of my new snaha? So headstrong. And we have to live together, cook in the same kitchen."

Doonya spotted me openly listening, jabbed Mable in the ribs, jerked her head toward me. They left the kitchen, talking low.

Loud voices broke out directly overhead in Marusa's bedroom. Aunt Florence's sounded mad. I dropped the pans in the sink, went through the living room, past guests who lolled on couches and chairs which were pushed back against the walls to make room for the dining tables.

Everyone was sleek and drowsy after the feast and looking forward to more feasting after the ceremony at Zarubins that night. They were discussing Maxim Dutoff's cow which had escaped from a nearby pasture and had just galloped through the village, Maxim in pursuit.

"A bawling cow means a bossy starushka," mother-in-law.

"Nyet, it means a willful snaha," daughter-in-law.

Peter's brothers were carrying the soondook out to the truck, followed by Peter's father with the tooke containing the bridal quilt. It would be placed on the groom's quilt by the mothers and the bed would look high and soft and inviting. Everyone would laugh and tease, and the bride and groom would blush, pretend they weren't interested, that they had loftier thoughts today.

Upstairs I skimmed along the corridor, past bedrooms with their tall narrow windows, spare whitewashed walls, where Marusa's grandparents and parents slept. And I thought it no wonder Marusa often complained everyone knew when she came in on a Saturday night, for each squeaky tiptoe, each cautious footstep could be heard on the creaking floorboards as she crept past all those disapproving doors.

The small commotion brewing around Marusa's door consisted of the bride, her aunt and her mother. Aunt Florence had her turkey look on. Face all red, neck long, saying in a loud voice that she was so ashamed, and to change right away and maybe just maybe not too much harm was done even though it would be all over town by Monday. Marusa was weeping, ruining her rouge, and my mother was standing ineffectually between them, clasping and unclasping her hands.

Then Marusa, who'd looked right through me at school and kept on talking to her friends, who'd ignored me during family visits unless she was bored and then taken me upstairs, told me ghosts were seen floating along the dim hallways, even told me I'd been a foundling abandoned by my real mother near the cemetary, suddenly became Marusa my friend. She reached out and took my hand.

In that instant, as we faced our mothers, I became her ally. Us against them. Cousins forever. I felt her cool fingers, the pressure of the unfamiliar wedding band.

"Yes. Wear what you want, Marusa. It's your marriage."

Was that me sounding profound and grown-up? Aunt Florence and my mother looked at me for the first time, not knowing what to make of this unexpected alliance.

"It's your wedding, after all."

"Ana," my mother had recovered. "It's none of your business, or mine either. I'm not going to take sides, Florence," she said, then turned to Marusa, "Although it will be easier on everyone if you give in to your mother, dear." Diplomatic. No one could ever get mad at my mother.

Marusa let go of my fingers, smiled at me as I said one last "do it," shrugged her shoulders.

I went downstairs, thinking I'd do the same someday. When my turn came, I wouldn't give in either. For I'd felt Marusa's strength. Through her I could reach my dreams, unformed as they were. Maybe I'd take the university program at school, go on to college. I wouldn't even marry before I was twenty. I could do as I wanted and Marusa had shown me how. She'd opened the door a crack and I had slipped through after her. And the best, most wonderful part of all was that she had turned to me.

"I am ready," a voice said, and there she was, in her traditional outfit, as demure as she'd looked at the zapoy. She searched the group of people around the steps, seeking approval, smiling when she found it. She didn't look at me.

I followed the crowd to the cars, my unformed dreams dying inside me.

It was fleeting, Marusa's independence. Just those few hours in the wedding gown when she lived her dream. And mine. For after the wedding, after the ceremonies and the feasting, she became a dutiful wife. Within a year she bore a son. Within five years, she had three little boys tugging at her while she shopped at the co-op.

Under Mable's tutelage, Marusa was becoming an expert cook, her pirahi pastry light, her borsch renowned. It was rumoured, according to Aunt Florence, that Marusa would eventually take over her mother-in-law's position as head cook at weddings and funerals.

Joey Valentine and the Show Pass

"We've got a new boy at school," Sara, two years my junior, said as she buttered a thick piece of crusty bread. "He just moved from Saskatchewan."

We were sitting around the kitchen table, eating homemade pea soup. The stove spit out crackling noises, making our house a haven in the chilly autumn evening.

"What's his name?" I asked the all-important question.

"Joey. Joey Valentine."

"I knew a Mary Valentine once, in North Ridge back in Saskatchewan," mama said. "Wonder if it's the same one."

"It's not a common name," papa said. "It might be her. Why don't you find out?" He held out his bowl for more soup.

Sara and I lost interest in the conversation when mama brought out her upside-down plum cake and fresh cream.

Next day at school, Sara said to me, "Look. That's him. Joey Valentine."

I saw a boy who was tall for his age, nearly as tall as me. Thin, almost fragile, with a scared, hungry look in his huge eyes. His fair hair hadn't been cut for a long time, a thick mat which stuck out around his face, making his head appear larger than it was. He wore one of those grey flannel shirts that the farm boys sometimes wore, although they usually dressed in plaid shirts. The town boys always wore v-necked sweaters or even shirts. Sometimes even their Boy Scout uniforms, but in summertime only, because of the shorts. We said they looked like sissies, but never to their faces. Joey's pants were too short for his growing legs, and the suspenders pulled them up even higher, and he had dusty boots, also shunned by the town boys who usually wore running shoes. He saw me looking at him and turned away, scowling. I decided I didn't like him.

"Teacher said Joey could be a good student if he applies himself," Sara said at supper that night.

"I wonder if he is Mary Valentine's boy," mama said, bringing out her homemade doughnuts. "His mother was a smart student too, even though she was a mouse, never speaking unless teacher asked a question. Her family lived north of us in the bush. Rock farmers, we called them. She married when she was still in school. He was much older ... a widower. Her way of escaping the farm, I suppose."

A few weeks later, mama said, "I saw Mary Valentine today. She is Joey's mother. She sure was surprised to see me ... didn't know we lived here."

"Where's her husband?" papa asked.

"She didn't say, and I wasn't about to ask," mama replied from the pantry where she was putting away groceries. "She spoke only of Joey. Sounds like there's just the two of them."

"Where're they staying?" My father took off his heavy work boots and sat down at the table with the *Weekly Herald*.

"A little two-room house down by the railroad station. She says it's not much, but the rent's real cheap. You know, she has a sister in town. That's why they ended up here."

"How's she supporting the boy, then?"

"Welfare, I guess. I sort of asked her that, but she wouldn't give me a direct answer. Don't blame her." Mama settled at the table with a cup of tea.

Sara said, between mouthfuls of apple, "Poor Joey, he has to wear that grey flannel shirt every day."

"What's wrong with a grey flannel shirt?" Lisa said.

"It's ugly, that's what," I said. "Hardly anybody wears one, except Joey. But then he doesn't suit anything but grey flannel. He doesn't fit in with the town kids, or the farm kids, either."

"Ana, you watch that tongue of yours. If you can't say something nice, don't bother saying anything at all," mama said. She often complained she couldn't figure out who I took after. Perhaps papa's great-aunt Varah. "You're just lucky you have a father who can buy you a new dress for Christmas and a summer dress besides."

It wasn't that I disliked Joey, or any of the other poor kids in school. In fact, I didn't hang out with the town kids either. We weren't poor, but our little clapboard house and our carpenter father in his old pickup, didn't compare to the large white houses, and with fathers who owned the drugstore or the hardware store and who drove to work in a shiny De Soto or Mercury car. And I didn't play with the kids who lived in those shabby houses down by the tracks either. Houses whose yards were strewn with broken bits of toys, tin cans and dog excrement. Where children and skinny cats and dogs fought in the alley and mothers screamed from doorways, or walked about looking pale and exhausted. Most of my friends lived on the little farms around our place.

Sara on the other hand was more tolerant and had friends everywhere. "Teacher said yesterday Joey's marks are good, and he might make top student this term," she said.

The show pass was a big event in our school. The top student in each class received a free pass to all the movies at the Regal Theatre. The rest of us were envious, because we couldn't afford a movie more than once or twice a month. So, old clothes or not, Joey might be going to the movies several nights a week and to the exciting cowboy shows at the Saturday matinee besides.

Autumn passed, and Mrs. Valentine visited us. She never had mama over, because she didn't want mama to see what we supposed was her shabby little house.

Mrs. Valentine was a small, thin woman, who looked years older than my mother. Her scraggly, light brown hair was swept back in a little unkempt bun, and her pale eyes were hidden behind thick glasses. She always wore a long, brown coat and carried a paper shopping bag with City Grocery printed on it.

Mama would bring out her everyday tea set and some kalachy, the huge, soft cookies she always baked, open up a jar of raspberry preserves, and they would talk. Rather, mama would talk, and Mrs. Valentine would listen, nodding and sometimes making a remark in her small colourless voice. She would leave before papa came home, always with vegetables or fruit from the cellar, which my mother tucked in the shopping bag, waving away the feeble protests.

"What do you talk about?" papa asked one day.

"You sure don't have much in common."

"Oh, we reminisce about school and people we knew in North Ridge, but mostly we talk about our children. She's worried that Joey's not fitting in with the rest of the kids ... wishes she could afford better clothes for him. You know how kids are at this age. They judge you by what you wear. But she's had a bit of luck. She just got a job cleaning the Stargate Café after hours. She says she hates the long walk home after midnight because it's so cold, and she hates leaving Joey at night even more. Sometimes he stays at her sister's place, but she doesn't like doing that too often. Her sister's husband's a complainer. But the money sure comes in handy, she says."

Sometimes Joey came with his mother, but this proved painful to all concerned. He didn't talk to us, just sat in the big armchair in the living room, reading his book. Sara and I ignored him, even though mama pleaded with us to play with him, show him the dog, the cow and chickens. But we always went upstairs to our room. Sara especially was shy because he was in her class and it was one thing to be friendly at school, but if anyone found out he was at our house, he'd be labelled her "boyfriend". And we would absolutely die if one of our friends came over to play and saw him. He with his grey flannel shirt and old boots. We'd just die! It would be all over school next day that Joey Valentine visited the Katelnikoff girls.

So we tolerated his presence, but underneath there was envy, because he'd been named top student that winter, and could attend all the movies he wanted.

It was Sara who first told me about the change in Joey. "He's wearing a plaid shirt and new shoes."

I couldn't imagine Joey in anything but grey flannel.

I saw him at school next day and hardly recognized him. He was wearing a bright blue sweater and pants that fit. Catching my look, he quickly turned away.

"Mama, Joey's wearing new clothes now. He looks as nice as the other boys," I said one Saturday morning. I was helping my mother bake a marble cake, making molasses swirls in the pale yellow batter.

"Maybe his father's sending money, and high time too. Or maybe Joey's aunt gave him clothes for Christmas. Of course, there's not much money in that quarter, either. I'm glad he looks nice. He's such a good, polite boy."

One evening, I was sitting in the living room, reading. The house was quiet, except for the battery radio which was playing softly. Supper dishes were finished and my parents were in the adjoining kitchen. I heard the clink of china and tea being stirred.

"Don't want the girls to hear this," papa began, "Where are they anyway?"

I turned off the Hit Parade and leaned forward in the overstuffed armchair. *Anne of Green Gables* slid to the floor.

"In their rooms reading, more than likely," mama said. "What is it? What's going on?"

"Well, I was in Statler's Dry Goods today, buying some new coveralls. Tim Statler looked a little upset. Said since we're pretty good friends, he wanted to tell me something, but he didn't want it to go any further."

Now I was really listening.

"Tell me. What was it?" Mama's voice was getting impatient.

"I know you're not going to like this, Katya," he began, "but it's about Mary Valentine."

"What about Mary Valentine? I haven't seen her for

a while. Is she all right?"

"She's fine healthwise. It's this other thing, dammit. Tim Statler said she's been coming into his store for quite some time now. Not buying much, mostly looking over the boys clothing, and putting it back. Well, a while ago, he was in his office. You know it's above the store area, and he can look down and see everything. So, he was sitting up there and he saw Mary come in. She walks right over to the boys clothing and starts looking at the shirts and sweaters. Then she looks around and quick as a wink shoves this shirt from the counter into her shopping bag."

"Oh no ..."

"Betty, his sales clerk, is none too bright, so she don't notice anything." Papa paused, and I could hear him refilling his teacup. I was hardly breathing.

"Well, what happened next?" Mama asked, but her voice sounded funny, as if she didn't really want to know.

"Well, nothing. Tim thought of going down and confronting her, with the goods on her and all. But then he thought of the boy, and her with no man to support her, and how proud she is. So he just let that one go by."

"That was real decent of him," mama said in a tight voice. "You said 'that one'. Was there another time?"

"Well, yes. The same thing happened again about a week later. Only this time it was a pair of pants. He had no choice but to go down and confront her."

"Oh my God! How did she take it? Did he get the police?"

"No, he just talked to her. Said he'd seen her take the pants. She didn't say a word. Just looked at him. He couldn't see her eyes behind those funny, thick glasses of hers. Then she reached in her shopping bag and got the pants out and laid them on the counter. Then she turned around and walked out of the store with her head up, still without saying a word."

"Oh, that's just awful. I feel so sorry for her," mama's voice broke.

"So do I. But Tim had no choice. You can't have that sort of thing going on."

"I know she did it for Joey. She was so worried she couldn't provide for him properly. Oh, I wish I could talk to her, tell her I understand. That I'm her friend, no matter what. But she's so proud."

A chair was pushed back. I musn't let anyone see me. Picking up my book, I tiptoed across the braided rug.

"Ana, what are you doing?" Papa's stern voice.

I stopped in the doorway, didn't turn. "Reading."

"What did you hear?"

I stared at the wall.

"Answer me."

"I heard ... you and mama ... talking."

"Ana, you were eavesdropping," mama said.

"I'm sorry."

"You must promise not to tell anyone what you just heard. Promise me."

"I promise."

"We'll not talk of this again," Papa said. "You may go now."

I went up the stairs, looked into Sara and Lisa's room. Sara was on the bed, reading, Lisa playing with her paper dolls. I lay on my bed, thinking about the Valentines. I'd felt sorry for them because they were poor, but Mary Valentine was a thief, and she hadn't been punished. And now Joey went to all the movies. It wasn't fair.

I saw Joey at school, but we ignored each other. We'd never been friends, even though I'd felt a bit sorry for him. Now I was consumed with curiosity. I had never known anyone whose mother was a thief. Somehow it seemed even worse to have your mother steal rather than your father. I couldn't imagine my mother stealing anything. She didn't even let us take a grape from the open bins in the co-op.

The spring report cards were coming, and Sara was working hard. She desperately wanted to win that show pass. I coached her in spelling, and Papa went over her arithmetic each night. We knew she had a good chance.

"It would be nice to win, dear," mama would say. "But winning isn't everything."

"You should win," I'd tell Sara when we were alone. "You deserve it more than Joey."

I was an average student, but Sara had inherited papa's quick mind with figures and mama's remarkable memory. Each term she'd come in third or fourth, but this was the first time she had a chance to win anything, at school or at home. I was the firstborn. Always got the new clothes and when I outgrew them they got passed down to Sara. I was the first to start school, Sunday School and Russian School. By the time Sara got around to anything, I had already done it. Lisa was the baby with her golden wavy hair and fragile air. She whined and pouted and charmed her way around our parents, easy tears filling the blue eyes.

But it was Sara, sturdy brown-haired Sara, shorter and broader for her age than Lisa and myself, who was philosophical and stoic, and stubborn when she wanted something. And she wanted that show pass.

So we all coached Sara, through the soft spring

evenings, when we longed to be skipping rope or playing hopscotch. I resented giving up my playtime, but I knew that if Sara won that pass, I'd have to accompany her to the movies.

The tension was evident each night at supper, when someone would casually ask how the others were doing and if they were studying as hard.

"No," Sara would answer. "Maybe Joey is, though. He knows all the answers in class, and his lessons are always right."

"So are yours." Papa would say.

It seemed all our conversation centred around Sara's winning that award. Even the kids at school were discussing it, and everyone was hoping Sara would come out on top. She was friendly and pretty. Joey, on the other hand, was an enigma. No one knew very much about him, and no one cared. He was merely the spoiler.

Exams were over and we had to await the results which arrived on report card day. That morning Sara came down to breakfast wearing her best school clothes. Navy pleated jumper and long sleeved white blouse with eyelet-trimmed collar, red knee socks, her Christmas patent leather shoes. She'd slicked her straight brown bob with Vaseline Hair Oil, parted it on one side, anchored it with a red barrette on the other side. She beamed at us happily and suddenly I wanted to protect her.

I waited for Sara after school, but when she saw me, she burst into tears and ran past me.

"Sara, wait. Did you get it ... what's wrong?" I yelled, running after her.

"No, she didn't get it. Joey did," one of her classmates said. "But we all wanted her to win."

I slowly walked home, dreading the moment I'd have to face Sara and the rest of the family.

She took it harder than we expected. After the disappointment, my parents stated there would be other times.

"But I worked so hard. It should have been mine."

At school the following week, I caught a glimpse of Joey and resentment bubbled up in me. I knew I was unreasonable, but I wished that every bad thing in the world would happen to him.

Joey's mother was a thief. If everyone knew, they'd laugh at him and his show pass. It would serve him right.

At noon, I said to Martha, "Joey's new clothes sure look nice, don't they? Too bad they were stolen. His mother took them and didn't even pay for them. Still, he looks nice. Especially when he goes to the Regal Theatre all dressed up."

Martha's eyes widened as she took in my quickly whispered words.

"It may not be true, of course, but it's what I heard," I said, then hastened to add, "Don't say anything, please."

By after school, I'd accomplished my mission.

"Joey's got store-bought clothes, only they're not bought," the kids jeered when they saw him. It was as if they'd been waiting for this chance.

He stopped and looked questioningly at us.

"Hey Joe, didn't you know your old lady's a thief?" one of the older boys asked.

"A thief," several chanted. "She takes clothes from the store and you wear them."

Joey's face turned a vivid red. "That's not true."

"It's true. You're wearing them now," the chants

continued.

"I am not. You're liars ... all of you." He turned and ran, and I saw a glint of tears in his eyes, and I wondered at that moment if I should have said anything at all, then decided not to worry. Joey was put in his place and this would be the end of it.

That night Sara recounted the incident.

"Don't you girls tease Joey," mama said. "He's our friend."

"How did they find out?" I heard her ask papa that evening.

"I don't know," he replied. "Was it you?" His voice was stern.

"Of course not. As if I'd say anything. Mary's my friend." I could hear the indignation in her voice.

"Well, then, Tim Statler must have told someone. Or Betty, his clerk. She's not too swift, as I recall."

"What about Ana? She could have let it slip."

"She wouldn't — not after she promised. But I'll ask her," papa said. "Ana, come here."

I came out of the living room, hoping I looked innocent and untroubled.

"Ana, did you tell anyone about Mrs. Valentine?"

"No." I answered quickly. Not too quickly, I hoped.

"Are you sure? Think."

"I'm sure, papa," praying I'd be forgiven for lying.

"Well, as long as it wasn't one of us," mama said.

I felt a hot shame. For telling everyone about Joey, and for lying to my parents.

Next day the kids were still talking about it, only now they had no victim. Joey had stayed away. He didn't show up the next day, or the following one. I was a bit uneasy.

"Joey's quit school, I think," Sara said.

Saturday morning, mama walked across town to Mary Valentine's house to see if Joey was sick and if she could help. I hung around home, waiting for her, and it wasn't until late afternoon when I finally saw her walk up the path, and I scanned her face anxiously, my mouth dry. For a moment I thought she'd been crying. Then she saw me in the window and smiled, and I relaxed. Everything was fine.

I opened the door.

"What happened? Is everything okay at Joey's house?"

She looked at me for a long moment, and I saw the tears in her eyes.

"Mama, what is it? What happened?"

"Joey's run away, and Mary's so terribly upset. She hasn't had word from him since Tuesday. He didn't leave a note ... nothing. Didn't take extra clothes. He left for school as usual Tuesday morning, and everything seemed all right, but he never showed up after school. She waited and waited all that evening, praying he'd come, finally talked to her sister's girl who told her the kids were teasing Joey about his mother stealing clothes for him. It was dark by then and she went all over town, calling him, but couldn't find him. Her sister's there, but she can't seem to do anything with her. Mary keeps saying it's all her fault."

"Are the police looking for him?" Papa asked later.

"Yes. They've sent out bulletins, questioned people. Mary's afraid something terrible has happened. Says the police checked the riverbanks and everything."

"Some busybody got wind of her indiscretion, and now the boy's paying for it. Why couldn't people leave well enough alone?" Papa said angrily.

I wondered what direction his wrath would take if

he ever found out my part in the whole mess. If Joey had jumped in the river and drowned, it would be all my fault. I slept poorly and couldn't eat, and my lack of appetite didn't pass unnoticed. Mama thought I had a severe case of spring fever, and tried all her home remedies on me, including the despised Blackstrap Molasses and Cod Liver Oil Treatment.

About a week after Joey's disappearance, I came home to find the house empty and cold and terribly still. There was a hastily pencilled note from our parents on the kitchen table, saying they had to go out and would be back before supper and to stay in the house. This was unusual because my mother was always home after school, the stove going and supper started. Sara and I walked around, not knowing what to do. Lisa began whining. I had a sick feeling my mother's absence had something to do with the Valentines.

After what seemed to be hours, we heard the truck drive up. Mama and papa walked in, their faces grave and tired. Mama had tears in her eyes.

"Girls, Joey's been found," she put her arms around us, as if she needed comfort.

My throat clogged up so I couldn't speak.

"Where, mama? Is he all right?" This from Sara.

"No. He's had an accident. Train."

"Oh, mama. What happened?" Again from Sara.

"He tried to jump out of a moving boxcar and fell. They had to ..." her voice dropped to a whisper and we strained to hear, "They had to amputate his leg." She didn't look at us.

"You mean ... they cut it off?" Sara said, horror in her voice.

Lisa began to whimper, not really comprehending.

"Yes, Sara. He's been riding the rails for days, not

knowing where to go. He didn't want to see his mother or anyone else."

"Where is he? In hospital?" I'd finally found my voice.

Papa spoke for the first time, "Yes, but not here." He named a town about a hundred miles away. "We drove her over this morning. He'll be in hospital a long time."

"Mrs. Valentine is very upset because Joey doesn't want to see her," mama said. "I hope he'll come around, because she's all he's got in the world." She took off her good coat and headed toward the kitchen, "You girls help me with supper."

I stood unmoving. Tears streamed down my cheeks.

My mother turned to look at me, "Ana, are you coming? Don't cry, he's alive, and that's the most important thing."

I remained silent, looking down at the floor.

"I know you feel bad about Joey. He's your friend. But he'll be all right in time."

"I'm not his friend. I told everyone his mother's a thief. I did it!" I screamed, shutting my eyes tight so I wouldn't have to look at the stunned faces, relieved to finally say the awful words out loud.

"Oh my God," mama said.

"Ana, is that true?" I had never heard my father use that tone.

"Yes, yes. I'm so sorry," I shouted, still not looking at them.

"How could you?" My mother said.

"I was mad at him for winning the pass, and I heard you and Papa talking, so I told," I said. "Are you going to tell Mrs. Valentine?"

"I don't know what good that will do," Papa said. He suddenly looked tired. "You'll have to live with it,

Ana. You've disappointed us greatly."

Sara looked at me wonderingly, and that hurt more than anything else. After all, I had done it for her. And now I was no longer the big sister who could do no wrong. Then she, too, went into the kitchen.

I could hear the homey sounds of cooking, the radio playing softly, yet I felt alone. For I had seen shame in the faces of my family.

That summer, after Joey recovered, he and his mother moved back to North Ridge, "where people are kinder to my boy." I didn't see them before they left.

But for a long time afterwards, I was haunted by nightmares of a large shadow chasing me, hopping on one leg, amazingly fast, a bloody sawed-off leg under its arm. It was always dark in the dream and I was running through woods, stumbling over stumps, branches whipping my face. And every time, just as the shadow reached me, I fell, looked into Joey's accusing eyes, and awoke. The dreams finally stopped. The guilt stayed.

And for the next three years, Sara won the show pass.

One day, about four years later, my mother mentioned that she'd talked to Joey's aunt who'd told her Joey was doing very well in high school. "Planning to attend medical school on scholarships," she'd said. "After all that time in the hospital, he made up his mind that's what he wanted. Always had the brains. Even won the show pass couple of times when he was here," she'd told mama.

"And Mary?" my mother had asked, "What about Mary?"

Mary was living on the farm in the bush. It was still in the family, "because they can't sell it ... too rocky. Joey lives with her until he goes to Saskatoon to the university. Then she'll be alone," the sister had said, then added, "She asks about your family when she writes. Says your girls were the only friends Joey had here."

The Selling

I was weeding onions in the hot sun when I saw the large silver De Soto glide to a stop in front of our house. A choking cloud of dust rose then settled over the dry grass and large, shaggy sunflowers, permeating every corner of our small cream-coloured house.

A tall, elegant woman emerged from the veil of dust, hesitated, then walked carefully toward me on very thin, very red high heels, which sank into the soft earth at each step. She wore a red hat and the cleanest, whitest dress I'd ever seen. No one I knew wore a hat in summer, unless you were weeding, and then it was a big straw hat.

Anglichka at our house. A rich one. Maybe she wanted directions to someone's farm.

I dug my bare toes into the cool earth and hoped she wouldn't notice the dirt-caked jeans.

"Hello, my dear. Is your mother home today?"

She was so thin, so stylish, that for a second my tongue went dry and stuck to the roof of my mouth.

I stared at her red earrings, which were not allowed at our house, papa being old-fashioned.

"No, mama's helping baba wash wool for our new quilts."

I took off my straw hat and wiped my perspiring forehead, shifted my hoe nervously, looked at her blonde waves, the crowsfeet around her eyes and mouth. Close up she looked older than mama. I figured she must be at least forty.

"I'm Mrs. Todhunter. I'm interested in buying some of your beautiful Doukhobor handicrafts. Do you have quilts or rugs or those pretty embroidered headshawls? I'll pay you well."

"Mama doesn't have much. Just doilies she made for her hope chest and a couple of rugs which we use. Oh, and there's Great-Grandmother Kootnekoff's beautiful linen towel. She spun it herself from her own flax. It's mama's favourite. All her cousins wanted it."

"It sounds just lovely, dear. May I please see it?"

"Well … all right."

Mama would be furious if she knew I'd taken a stranger into the house when it wasn't tidied up. I led the way into the kitchen, with its swarms of whining mosquitoes, smells of yesterday's borsch and sour milk. We didn't own a refrigerator. Didn't even have electricity yet.

"There." I pointed at the wall above the kitchen table where the towel hung. It was creamy white with a fine red border, and was draped carefully to show it off. I took it down and removed the cellophane covering.

"It's the dust," I said. "With the road so close and all."

Mrs. Todhunter took the towel and held it up, examining the finely-turned hem, the lace edging.

"It's just lovely. I'll give you three dollars for it." She emphasized the 'three'.

"Three?" I repeated in amazement. Who would pay three dollars for a piece of cloth? An old piece of cloth.

"Why, isn't that enough? You are quite the little bargainer, you know." She pouted, then laughed, her red mouth stretching up and around large blue-white slightly buck teeth, smeared with scarlet lipstick. "Okay, how about five then? I simply must have it. I will spread it out on my sideboard. It will set off my silver tea service perfectly." She leaned toward me, said confidingly, "I just inherited that tea service from my mother-in-law, you know. And I sure worked hard to get it. Had to be nice to her for twenty years. But it was worth it."

"Mama might not want to part with the towel. It was her baba's." I wanted to be assured I was doing the right thing.

Mrs. Todhunter looked at me measuringly, narrowed her eyes slightly, then laughed again, "Six dollars then. And a whole dollar for your trouble."

"All right." I was convinced my mother would be pleased. Money was scarce.

Mrs. Todhunter took a large roll of money from her purse and peeled off several bills. She picked up the towel, winked at me and left, trailing a delicious perfume.

Probably Evening in Paris, I thought. Not Jergens Lotion like my mother used.

I put a dollar in my pocket and the rest in mama's pink Depression Glass sugar bowl. It had been her wedding present, and used only for Sunday company.

I sat down in the kitchen to ponder what to do with my dollar — the most money I'd ever owned all at once in my whole life. Saturday matinees for two whole months. Or, if I went for one month, I'd be able to buy a dozen jawbreakers to suck on during each matinee. It was a difficult decision.

A short time later, I heard our old green Chevrolet

pickup groan into the yard, doors slam, and voices of my parents and sisters.

"Hello Ana. Onions weeded already? You should have started on the potatoes then." Mama walked in, carrying a bag of freshly washed wool. We'd have new quilts this winter.

"Close the screen door," papa said. "Kamaree are real bad today."

"Mama ... Guess what? You know that old towel of baba's?"

"Of course," she said, reaching for kindling, opening the door of the cookstove, twisting a page of the Home Loving Hearts section of the *Free Press Weekly* and lighting it. Soon my mother would be swooning in the overwhelming heat as she stirred the big pot of halooshki, the vegetable and dumpling soup, which we ate along with pieces of raw onion and thick slices of bread and butter.

"Of course I know it. It's the prettiest thing I have. A real family treasure. And someday, it will be yours. Babushka made it, you know, for her hope chest when she was still in Russia." She looked up from lighting the stove, "Why ... where is it? Did you take it down?"

"Mama — that's what I'm trying to tell you. I sold it," I beamed proudly.

"Sold it?" She slowly stood up, frowning at me.

"Yeah. I got six dollars for it and a dollar for my trouble."

I reached into the pink sugar bowl and handed her the money.

"A lady in a white dress and the highest heels I ever saw drove into our yard. And she bought the towel. You should just see her silver car and her red hat, and she had earrings to match her hat and shoes and everything. She was a real glamour gal."

"Who is she?" My mother was frowning at me.

"Mrs. Todhunter, she said. But don't worry. I've already got the money. See?"

"You sold my baba's towel?"

"But I thought you'd be happy. Now we can all go see that Doris Day movie. Tho whole family can go together, and we can all have popcorn too. Or ..." as she continued to stare at me, "You can spend it all on a new Gibson Girl blouse. They have some cute ones in the co-op."

"You sold my prized possession!" Mama's face, usually cheerful and smiling, had angry lines on the forehead. Her voice was high and shrill — a danger signal. I backed toward the doorway and into my father who had just walked in.

"Take me to town. To the Todhunter place," she said. "It's that big yellow house with the tower and the stained glass windows."

She didn't look at me as they walked outside, just muttered to Sara to watch the stove.

I began peeling potatoes and onions for the halooshki, avoiding Sara and Lisa's curious eyes, and half an hour later, mama walked in with the towel over her arm. She hung it in its usual place over the table.

Finally she turned and looked at me. "It cost me ten dollars. I had to practically beg that woman for it."

The remainder of that summer, while my friends spent the hot afternoons swimming in Lyman's Pond, I could be found weeding the garden, shovelling out the cowbarn or chicken coop, and babysitting Mrs. Nichvolodoff's terrible twin boys for twenty-five cents a day, and putting my earnings into mama's pink Depression Glass sugar bowl.

A Dead Village without Children

The bus inched around the tight bend, hugging the mountain. Outside, fog nearly obliterated the landscape. The wipers were working overtime, a losing battle against the enormous flakes of wet snow. Despite the packed bus, it was warm and cosy inside as people dozed or watched the tiny TV screen up front.

In Penticton, a tall, slender woman got on, sat down beside me. Jeans, brown melton wool jacket and boots. The rich brown of her jacket matching her thick dark hair and eyes. The only time I'd seen hair that particular mahogany colour was during another bus ride, another season.

"Hideous weather, isn't it," I said, searching her face for a familiar smile, a look.

"Yes. It's awful when the airport's fogged in. I hate buses."

Faint accent. I peered in the semi-darkness, noted the white strands in the springy hair, which confirmed that she was around my age.

"Have we met ... when we were very young maybe?"

The woman searched my face, then leaned back, looked ahead, "I don't think so."

I caught the inflection.

"Did you ever live in the Kootenay Valley?" I said.

"Why yes. How did you know?"

"And is your name Lara?"

"Yes, but I don't know you."

"I think it's your eyes and hair. It's such an unusual colour. And I caught the accent."

She frowned slightly, but remained silent.

"My name's Ana." As usual, I was talking too fast when I wasn't sure of myself. "And I've lived there all my life. Still do in fact."

"Did I know you well?"

"No. We met only two or three times. But I remember you and I've often wondered what happened to you." I paused, then added, "The last time I saw you was at the courthouse."

For a moment I thought she hadn't heard me. Then she said quietly, "I remember the courthouse. And I remember you."

I was leaning back on the sticky, cracked leather seat, reading *True Love* magazine, eating red licorice, as the Greyhound bus huffed and creaked up the hills and around hairpin bends. It was hot, as only a day in late August could be. A muggy, sticky, farewell-to-summer kind of hotness. Outside the open window, the air was scented with pine trees and dry weeds and hot rocks. Inside, there were smells of perspiring bodies, overripe fruit and stale bologna sandwiches.

I shifted uncomfortably, trying to find a cool spot on the warm leather. There was none.

I'd been on the bus since five a.m., travelling from New Westminster, where I'd left my great-aunt Helen at her sister Elsie's small stuccoed house.

"Let Ana come with me. I don't understand English so good. I'll pay her way."

"I don't know," my mother had said, "She's never been away."

"I'll pay her way back, too."

And that settled it. Aunt Helen needed me to tell her what the bus driver meant when he hollered "all aboard" and "where's your ticket" and to read the greasy menus at the smoky bus depots, although she invariably ordered no-meat soup and tea.

After two days in New Westminster, where I'd been taken on a fast sightseeing trip to the Army and Navy and to the airport at Lulu Island, I was on my way home with a bag of devilled-egg sandwiches, which I left in Chilliwack. Who wanted to eat a bag lunch when I could eat in bus depot cafés, daringly buying the magazine, being careful not to talk to anyone except the driver.

In Penticton, a girl about my age got on, looked around at the nearly full bus, hesitated, then made her way toward the seat beside me. She sat down, drew her cotton floral skirt around her knees, being careful not to touch me. Her ticket stub was clutched tightly in her hand, but I could see her destination — my home town.

I kept sneaking looks at her, at the big dark eyes, the twin mahogany braids, then pushed self-consciously at my limp blonde hair. I'd carefully curled it in rags the night before, but it had gone straight before I'd even reached Hope.

After watching her sideways over the pages of my magazine, I finally said "hi."

She gave me a startled look followed by a faint "hi," and more rearranging of skirts, feet planted neatly side by side, ladylike.

"My name's Ana. Ana Katelnikoff. What's yours?"

"Lara Hoodicoff." So faint, I had to lean toward her to hear.

I felt an immediate kinship.

"What school do you go to?"

To my surprise, I sensed a shrinking, a sort of drawing back.

"Central School," fainter yet.

"Well so do I. What grade are you in?"

"I ... what grade are you?"

"Grade eight this September."

"I'm grade seven."

"How come I haven't seen you at school?" I'd remember that hair, those eyes.

"I ... I'm just moving. From Penticton ..."

"Penticton. Gee, you're lucky." I looked at her with respect. "I sure wish I lived in a big town like Penticton ... went to school there."

I couldn't wait to tell my friends about Lara.

She didn't say anything, and a few minutes later, when I looked over at her, she had closed her eyes.

And then we were pulling into another small town, another bus depot with it's smoky café and washrooms with two toilet stalls, one free and one where you put a nickel in the door handle before you could go in, only no one ever did, just held open the door for the next person, or like me, crawled under the door if no one was looking.

In the coffee shop, I slid onto the seat across from Lara, scanned the stained menu.

"I think, the special," I said to the hovering, gum-chewing waitress.

"You?" The waitress swivelled toward Lara, looked over her thick-lashed eyes and shiny hair, said with envy, "Well, make up your mind. Bus won't be here all day."

"Same," Lara mumbled.

Our grilled cheese sandwiches, french fries on the side, arrived and we were occupied with pouring out ketchup, dipping sandwiches and fries, glistening with hot fat, into the crimson globs.

And then the driver came in, hollered "All aboard," and we went out into the blistering sunlight and climbed onto the creaking, gas-fumed bus.

The combination of food and being awakened at four a.m. made me sleepy, and as I sank into oblivion, I handed Lara my magazine, "Read 'Burning Hearts'. It's really sad."

The crying baby two rows back jolted me awake. I surfaced slowly, drowsily watched Lara through my lashes. She turned the pages of the magazine, looking at pictures.

"Did you like it — the story — did you cry? I did."

She said in a matter-of-fact voice, "I'm not supposed to read trash," and handed me the magazine.

And a few minutes later, brakes protesting, tin body shaking, the bus squeeled into the Stargate Café and Bus Depot and shivered to a stop.

I saw my mother's anxious face as I stepped down. To my dismay, she enveloped me in her arms, looking relieved. I quickly glanced around to see if anyone had noticed this embarrassing display, but Lara had disappeared. I stuffed the magazine into a trash can.

My mother and I walked home through the sun-baked town, and past the big, cool, verandahed white houses, past the little cottages on the outskirts, and on to the country to the little farms with their huge vegetable gardens, the inevitable cow tethered in the shade.

She carried the family suitcase, a small brown imitation leather, wallpapered inside, and I had the Aylmer soup box tied with twine. It contained four pairs of new, sadly outdated shoes which Aunt Helen had bought at the Dollar Forty-Nine Sale at Army and Navy.

"School shoes for you girls and a pair for your mother."

We stopped often, to rest in the shade and to shake the sand out of our sandals, and all the while I thought about Lara and her cool manner and I was proud to have a friend from a glamorous place like Penticton with its golden summer beaches, its green rows of sun-ripened orchards. I compared our cottonwoods and evergreens, small river, the town with the co-op at its heart. A town everyone wanted to leave in summer, not visit.

The next time I saw Lara, she was accompanied by a tall woman with weather-beaten face, dressed in traditional Doukhobor clothing, full gathered skirt and long-sleeved blouse, fringed shawl on her head. I recognized her, knew she lived in a village of small, unpainted houses, in the hills outside of town. The same faith as me, yet different.

Suddenly, everything was clear. Lara was Sons of Freedom. That's why she didn't read the story. She couldn't. And she didn't live in Penticton. She was probably visiting relatives there who were working in the orchards for the summer.

That day I was with my friends Zina and Marion. I'd told them all about my new friend, and especially about her having lived in the Okanagan. I'd even hinted she'd invited me to visit her relatives there during school holidays. It wasn't true, but it gave me an aura of glamour that long boring summer.

We were in Murphy's drugstore, supposedly buying school supplies, but more interested in lipstick and perfume. Lara and the woman were over by the pharmacy and I could hear Lara interpreting. I often did it for my baba even though I didn't like speaking Russian in front of an Angleek. However, Lara seemed at ease as she talked to the pharmacist in her polite voice, then turned to the woman and spoke softly in rapid Russian.

As she turned toward the druggist, she saw me, smiled and said shyly "Hi Ana." The woman looked over at me, a penetrating unsettling kind of look.

"Hi," I looked past Lara and her smile faded.

"Who's that? Is she the friend you told us about?" asked Zina.

"Yeah. She's still visiting in town."

"Oh yeah? She lives in that village. Is that where you're going for your holidays?" Marion and Zina were delighted.

I'd been feeling smug about being in New Westminster and riding the bus home all by myself and meeting a new friend from a place we were dying to visit, while they had spent the summer at home, pulling weeds and milking cows.

Anger welled up in me, at my friends who were now poking each other and making silly snickering sounds, but especially anger at Lara for her deception.

I sneaked a glance at Lara, who was smiling uncertainly. I gave her my best narrow-eyed hostile glare, then deliberately turned away. When I looked again, she was following the woman out the door, head down.

"Ona cheeyah?" Who is she? I heard the woman ask as the door closed behind them.

I looked at Marion and Zina for approval, but they had already forgotten Lara.

A month into the school year, I was walking past the big stone courthouse, on my way downtown to get sewing supplies for my Home Ec project.

"The easiest pattern you can find, Ana," Mrs. Porterhouse had said. "You're all thumbs. And those dirty little knots you make when you baste. And the uneven hems. Thank goodness you don't have to take sewing next year."

I was so engrossed in thinking about my navy slub rayon material — "It's serviceable, Ana," my mother had said. "I've had it in the trunk for years, and now I have a use for it," and the soft, filmy pastel dresses Zina and Marion were creating, "flocked nylon ... ideal for parties" — that I didn't see the little group of people until I was in the middle of them.

I was surprised when I saw the RCMP officers herding three children, two girls and a boy, toward the courthouse. The children walked quietly, with scared, uncertain looks on their faces. My surprise turned to numbing shock when I saw that Lara was one of them. At that moment she saw me.

"Hi," I croaked. I didn't know what else to say.

"Hi." It came out automatically.

And as I watched them climb the stone steps of the courthouse, I thought that Lara reminded me of a wooden puppet, Howdy Doody — stiff body, stiff face, mouth moving, freckles standing out on her white face.

I forgot the sewing pattern, and hurried home. My father was already there, and we stood in the tiny kitchen, words tumbling out, supper forgotten.

"So they've done it," my mother said. "Government in Victoria threatened to take the kids if they didn't send them to school, and now they're keeping their promise. Thank God it isn't us."

"They're not the first," Papa said. "Hunting those kids down like animals. They come into their villages, searching houses, barns, fields." He shook his head, "Bozshi Moi. Kak zveree." My God. Like animals.

"Where are they taking them?"

"To New Denver they say, where the Japanese were sent during the war. They've still got the old t.b. sanitarium there and the children will be staying in it. So now New Denver has prisoners again. Only this time they're all children."

"This time it's Lara."

"Who is Lara?"

"A girl I met on the bus last month. She was the one I saw taken by the police today. What's going to happen to her? Why didn't she go to school, anyway?"

"Because, Ana, schools are run by the government and they say governments are evil … that war is taught there. Neither the parents or government would compromise." Then she added, "Of course, it's the children who suffer. Isn't it always the way?"

I knew what compromise meant, because our parents told us we weren't supposed to sing "God Save the Queen" or "O Canada" at school because the words spoke of allegiance to a woman and to a country and to "stand on guard," that we should stand up and be polite, just don't sing.

However, I felt guilty when we had to march around the chilly gymnasium to warm up. "Doukhobors don't march. Soldiers march," but on gym days, shivering in our skimpy shorts and singlets, we didn't explain to our young teacher from the sophisticated west coast, and to a group of girls who already thought we were different, why we weren't supposed to march. We were all trying to fit in, to belong.

As I lay in bed that night, staring at the branches swaying in the black wind outside, I thought of the hopeless, doomed look on Lara's face and felt guilty for snubbing her in the store. I pulled my covers tightly around me, hoping Lara was warm and safe, wherever she was.

In the weeks that followed, I kept thinking of Lara with her quiet dignity, of her mahogany hair, her grownup attitude. And I imagined her locked up for years, unable to live at home with her family, to go shopping downtown, to ride a bus through the mountains if she felt like it.

"There's even more demonstrations and violence against the government now," Papa said one evening.

And in the midst of the turmoil, more children from the villages in the hills were hunted down, taken to the dormitory, locked up, educated.

I thought that going to school like I did was lots easier.

"Were you taken to New Denver, Lara? Did you stay there a long time?"

"For four years, until I was fifteen," she looked out the darkened window into the snowstorm. "Sometimes I think I had no other life."

Lara had grown up in a tiny village in the mountains outside of town. The village consisted of small, drab, wooden houses and outbuildings on either side of a straggling dirt road. More villages were tucked away in the folds of the neighboring hills and in the lush, green valleys. There were no stores or service stations. Just the houses and barns and large vegetable gardens.

We had never met before that blistering day on the

bus, although our grandparents had all been together when they'd crossed the ocean at the end of the last century. Soon after they arrived, a small zealous group detached itself from the large group of Doukhobors and walked off across the prairie, saying they didn't believe in material goods or governments, and that they should spread Christ's teachings to all mankind.

Many families were separated, estranged forever.

"To this day, my cousin and I don't speak," my father would say.

Lara's family belonged to this small group of zealots, so it wasn't surprising we'd never met, until that day on the bus when she'd been visiting her parents in Penticton.

"They were picking peaches," Lara said, "but I had to stay with my aunt and help out. Besides there was no room in the little shack my parents were staying in. But I got to visit them and it was lovely, right in the middle of the orchard. No one knew us or bothered us, or laughed at us. And on my way home, I met you, Ana, and was afraid you'd turn against me when you knew who I was. So I lied, and then you saw us in the store and guessed.

"The government was threatening to take all children of school age. My aunt and uncle, they had a little boy ... well, they built a trap door in a closet in his bedroom, and my sister Dasha and Petya and I practised climbing up and down the ladder and sitting in the dark — 'As soon as the police come, run fast, don't stop. Climb down and be very, very still.'

"We'd practice hiding, huddled together in the darkness, giggling, listening to the sound of our breathing. I don't think we took it too seriously. After all, we were secure and this was Canada. So we watched every car driving into the village, and at night we had our clothes beside our beds.

"And then we heard about the children in one of the other villages. About the way the police just drove right in, got out of their cars carrying sticks, walked slowly toward the houses. There were about ten of them. Then the bus drove in. The people had come out of their houses by now, and when they saw the bus, they knew something very terrible was about to happen. Some were in the fields and came running.

"The police told the adults to stand to one side, and then lined up the children in a row on the other side, all the ones who looked of school age. The younger ones were clinging to older sisters and brothers. Some had no one to cling to. The door of the bus opened and the police herded all the children up the steps.

"By this time, the parents and grandparents were crying and shouting, mothers trying to get past the line of policemen, who stood in a row, arms extended at their sides, holding the sticks. They wouldn't let anyone through. The door of the bus closed and the bus rolled away down the hill, and the faces of the children were pressed against the windows. It all happened so quickly, the people had no time to do anything. They were too shocked. And then there was nothing but the silence. It was a dead village without children."

Lara's voice choked, stopped, then continued, "See ... it still bothers me. After all this time ..."

"You don't have to go on."

"No, I want to ... I need to talk about it. Soon after that it was my turn. And when it came, it too was a surprise. We thought we were ready, but the real thing is always so different. When the police car drove in that morning, I was in the kitchen doing breakfast dishes, my aunt and uncle were harvesting potatoes away from the house, and Petya and Dasha were playing in the yard. I didn't even hear the motor, just the voices, and looked out the window and saw the black and white car and I knew. So I dropped the towel and ran into Petya's room and hid under the trap door.

"As I sat there, barely breathing, heart nearly bursting, I could hear the policemen's voices, talking to Petya and Dasha. They were just eight and seven, you know. I kept waiting for Petya to yell for his mother, but all I heard were the men's voices. Then I heard the little ones crying, pleading.

"'No. I don't want to go. I want mama,' Petya's voice. And then I heard Dasha cry, 'Lara ... Lara. Help me.

"And before I knew it, I was out of that hole and running outside, and the police grabbed me, but not before the little ones threw their arms around me.

"We were seated in the back seat with a woman, and the two RCMP officers sat in front, and as the car rolled through the village, I looked back and saw my aunt running, shouting something. The car speeded up. We were taken to the courthouse and then on to New Denver that same day."

"That's when I saw you at the courthouse," I said. I had heard about New Denver, yet had never talked to anyone who'd stayed there. "How were you treated?"

"Oh Ana, we had good food and beds and learned to read and write, but imagine being separated from your family. Living without anyone who cared about you, just your little sister and cousin. And having to look out for them. When I arrived at the dormitory, it was late and they put us to bed. It was a huge building, all one floor. T-shaped, girls on one side, boys on the other.

Classrooms and dining hall in the centre. Petya cried because he wanted to sleep with us, but they took him away. He was very quiet after that. Next morning I was taken to see the matron and I was frightened and tried not to let her know how scared I was, so I stared out the window and wouldn't look at her. She thought I was rebellious and gave me a severe scolding about respect and how I should be grateful for this wonderful opportunity, for I would be taught not only reading and arithmetic, but manners. In fact, I'd be exactly like 'a well-bred little Englishwoman.'

"I didn't want to be a well-bred anything, especially an Anglichka. The other girls didn't like me because I was pretty and the boys talked to me. So I had no one except for Dasha and Petya."

"Didn't you see your family at all? They must have visited."

"Oh yes, the visits. The best and worst days in our lives. I still have bad dreams. Every other Sunday was Visitor's Day, and oh how excited I was the night before each visit. I couldn't sleep. But with the anticipation was pain. The pain of parting all mixed up with the joy of the visit. We'd be waiting by the fence long before our parents and grandparents arrived with picnic lunches. We'd kiss and touch each other through the wire fence, then stand back and hold a prayer service in Russian, reciting psalms, the Lord's Prayer, sing a hymn. Our mothers would take out the picnic lunch, pass eggs, tomatoes and cucumbers, cheese and bread through the fence. After we ate, we'd talk a little, but we knew the parting was coming fast and we wouldn't see one another for two whole weeks. And as the minutes of the visit quickly wound down, only pain remained until it filled my heart, my very breath, and I'd try to hold back the tears because my mother would be holding back hers. I'd try to be very brave and blink real hard to keep them in the back of my eyes while I kissed my parents through the fence and touched mama's hand. As they drove away, everyone waved and waved and finally I'd run inside and hide under my bedcovers and cry. Many would have swollen eyes at supper that night."

"Didn't you try to run away? I think I would have tried it."

"I couldn't leave my sister and cousin and they were too little to run. We'd have been caught for sure. But three of the older girls ran away. They got outside the compound somehow and hitched a ride before they were missed, then walked along the railroad because they knew the highway would be scoured. When they got home, their families dressed them in long skirts and their heads were covered with shawls and they were sent to the garden to weed. When the police came around, all they saw were some elderly women bent over their cabbages. After that they were taken deep into the woods where they lived in a tent and the neighbors brought them food, and they were never apprehended. But I will never believe that taking the children was the right way to solve the problem."

I remembered those turbulent times. Railways, bridges and powerlines destroyed. I remembered especially, one cold winter night when an orange glow lit up our livingroom, and when we looked out the window, we saw the fire across the river, and by the time we'd dressed and driven over, the hall where we prayed and attended Russian classes was an inferno, sending flames and sparks roaring toward the black sky, and people watched helplessly, the water they threw on the fire turning to ice in the frigid night. I remembered crying.

Remembered the anger I felt.

And now Lara was sitting beside me again after all these years.

"But it's over now," I said, "You can forget it. Everything's mostly peaceful now."

"Forget ... no. Because for me the hardest part was when I finally turned fifteen and was allowed to go home. I'd been waiting for this special day since I'd been brought in. I couldn't wait to sleep in my bed, eat in our kitchen at home, walk around the yard, even go to town to the stores with mama. But then the matron called me in.

"'Lara,' she said, and she looked so stern I was sure she'd cancelled my departure. 'Lara, you know your sister could be released today too. She can leave with you.'

"My heart swooped up with the biggest joy I'd ever known. Both me and Dasha arriving home together.

"'But,' her voice was an icy drip on my spine, 'You'll have to sign this form first.' She shoved the paper across the desk toward me.

"'All right.' Anything to get out of there. My clothes were already packed, and I anxiously shifted from one foot to the other. If we left right away, I'd be home in time for supper and mama might make my favourite cheese vareniki. Dasha loved them too. Yes, I was sure mama remembered. I could taste the soft pastry, smothered in melted butter and fried onions. And there'd be the borsch. It would be just the same.

"'Sign your name right there on the bottom line. Where it says 'I promise Dasha will attend public school when she leaves New Denver.' And you have to promise she attends school, Lara. It's up to you once you sign.'

"But, I can't. My mother and father might not want me to. It's their belief.

"'Think very carefully, Lara. If you sign, your sister will go home with you today and you'll be responsible for her attending school. If you don't sign, she'll remain in New Denver another four years. This time without you.'

"I stared at her, not sure I'd heard right, thinking that this was a bad dream. A minute ago I'd been so happy, and now I was faced with the decision of my life. If I signed, I'd be going against my parent's beliefs. If I didn't sign, Dasha would be left behind. It was my choice."

It was quiet on the bus. People murmured sleepily. Heavy, wet snow continued falling, the wipers ploughing a v-shape on the windshield. The ride on that creaky bus that long-ago blistering day was another lifetime.

"What did you choose, Lara?" I whispered.

"I chose the only way. I didn't sign."

The bus slid sideways slightly, righted itself, continued slowly down the mountain. The fog had finally lifted. Through the swirling darkness, we could see the lights of the city.

Lekarka

It was the time I stayed at my cousin Marusa's in the communal village. The time my mother went to the hot springs for her varicose veins, and I had to go to my aunt's because my parents thought I was too young to stay home alone, and I thought I was too old to go with them. My mother had suffered since Lisa's birth, six years before, and none of the home remedies, the whispered prayers and poultices, the lauden sprinkled on water or fire, had helped. Finally my mother went to see Dr. Tenholme. "Stay off your feet, Katya," and mama had laughed at that. "Three children, a hungry husband, cow to milk, chickens to feed. You can tell he's a man."

So it was decided a trip to the soothing mineral waters and mud baths of the hot springs might be the best medicine, and on their way out, my parents dropped me and my small cardboard suitcase at my aunt's village just outside of town.

The Doukhobor villages were built in a rectangle. Two huge brick houses on one side, wooden one-storied adjoining buildings on the other three sides. Everyone shared the courtyard with its grassy area, its wooden sidewalks flanked by a profusion of summer flowers.

Red poppies nodded beside the verandahs of the brick houses. The kitchen, spare and scrubbed, was the centre of family life. Upstairs, leading off the long hallway, were many little bedrooms, and it was here I slept with my cousin Marusa in her narrow bed.

"You get the wall because you're company," and I didn't know if it was treat or punishment, as I didn't get a wink of sleep, just lay and listened to Marusa's light snores and endured her kicks. I finally dozed off as the pale light crept into the whitewashed room.

My aunt woke us by shouting up the stairs two or three times and finally we pulled on our clothes and stumbled down the narrow staircase to the enormous kitchen with the long table, where everyone was already seated. Marusa's aunt, uncle and cousins and her grandparents on her father's side, were assembled around the table, waiting. We walked over to the washstand in the corner and quickly splashed water on faces and hands. Marusa's grandfather was already reciting a shortened version of the Lord's Prayer. Aunt Florence brought out the huge pot of porridge ... it was her turn to cook that week ... and I tried to look enthusiastic.

"Devkee," she said as she ladled out the sticky mass. "We've just decided to go to the Declaratsiya celebrations in Brilliant. We'll be back Sunday night so you should be all right here. Or maybe I should stay behind?" But she sounded wistful. For Declaratsiya was old friends, mass singing, and plenty of good food. A reaffirmation of beliefs celebrated in mid-summer.

"Oh mama ... we'll be just fine. We'll hang around and visit. It's too hot to do anything else. Maybe we'll go down to the river and cool off."

"We'll even do some weeding," I said, avoiding Marusa's glare.

"If you need anything, just ask the neighbours in the village. You won't be afraid staying all alone in this big house?"

"The neighbours are right across the courtyard. It's not like we're isolated."

"Pah Rooskee, Devkee," speak Russian, girls, Marusa's baba said, then added that we'd forget our own language if we continued to chatter in English.

We nodded respectfully, looked down at our bowls.

I didn't like Marusa's grandmother very much. She was strict and thin as a whippet, bent over her badeek, walking stick, and forever scolding. So different from my own baba who was comfortable and warm, despite her efforts to mold us into accomplished young Doukhobor women.

An hour later, we stood on the dusty road lined with hollyhocks and waved at the overloaded car and pickup truck as they drove away to the annual summer celebration. Marusa and I looked at each other and smiled. Freedom. From being told to speak Russian. From household chores. From trying to cover our knees with our skirts when Marusa's grandmother was around.

Aunt Florence leaned out the window. "Remember, stay in the village. And Marusa, if you need anything, just ask Voykins. They said they'll watch out for you." She looked excited, her thoughts already on the pleasures of reunions and picnicking under cool shady trees, with the sounds of the ancient hymns and psalms echoing throughout the surrounding mountains.

"What do you want to do now, Ana?"

"Let's take a walk around the village. I've never been at the back."

"There's not much there. Just the barns and banya," steambath.

We walked behind the houses, past the sheds housing farm equipment, skirted gardens with their sunflowers, their enormous blue green cabbages and fragrant dill weed, ready for countless pots of borsch, around the banya where smoke drifted out of the chimney in anticipation of the weekly ritual of the bath.

"Well, have you seen everything? I told you there's not much."

"What's that little house over there?"

It was set apart almost like it didn't belong to the village. Old log walls overgrown with trees and bushes, bright blue door, sunflower plants nodding gigantic golden heads over the shaggy path. Scarlet geraniums in coffee cans in the two front windows. Cobwebby lace curtains ... was that a face in the dimness?

"That's where the babka lives. She used to be a lekarka, a medicine woman. A long time ago she healed people when they got sick or when they had the fright and wet the bed or stuttered. But now, Ana," Marusa's eyes gleamed wickedly, "she has the evil eye."

"I don't believe in the evil eye," I said, shivering in the warm sun.

"She can put a curse on you right from her window."

Marusa started running and I ran to catch up to her, afraid to look back in case the bapka was chasing us.

As we made the circle around the village and came back into the courtyard, we saw Voykins' pickup truck driving down the road followed by two cars.

"They all decided to go to Brilliant." An old man was leaning against the log fence, holding his wooden badeek in his gnarled hands. He spoke Russian, like most of the older people, "And if I were younger, I would be going too. Once I was the best singer and could recite every psalm. 'Na peerehdee, Teemonya. zavadee steeh,'" he said. Stand in front, Teemonya , start the hymn. "Now I stay behind, watch the stoves like an old woman." His watery blue eyes were sad. "Da, everyone gone but you and me devooshkee." He slowly began walking toward the steambath, leaning heavily on his badeek.

"The old woman in the house. He forgot about her."

"She doesn't count. No one hardly sees her, except Voykins when they bring her groceries from the co-op."

Marusa grinned suddenly. "Well, what shall we do? Go to town, see the matinee at the Regal?"

"We promised your mother."

"Don't be such a baby. She won't know." Marusa, several years older, was already used to minor deceptions.

"Can we use the banya first? Get the steam really going?" I was stalling, not keen on going to town and perhaps meeting Marusa's friends who either made sarcastic little comments or ignored me completely.

"As soon as Teemonya finishes his bath," she sighed, deciding reluctantly to be a gracious hostess.

It was quiet in the house, the spotless kitchen redolent with borsch, fruit tarts, whitewashed walls. We got out towels, clean underwear, fixed a sandwich and walked toward the banya, giving Teemonya time to get his pale, bent limbs washed and dried off, and dressed again in his suspendered black pants, the long sleeved shirt. We watched him step outside, leaning on the badeek, his body looking even thinner, boiled out by the steam, the clothes looser than when he went in.

Once inside the banya, we dropped our clothes on a bench, avoiding looking at each other's bodies, then put more wood in the stove. Marusa ladled out water, threw it on the hot rocks around the stove and billows of steam hissed and spat and rose in the tiny room, stinging my lungs. We climbed up on the top bench, slapped our legs and arms with twig switches to get our blood moving.

"If it were winter, we'd roll in the snow."

As I spoke, I reached over, gave Marusa's legs a smack with the twigs.

"Oh … this will get your blood moving," she yelled, hitting me back with her switch.

We were smacking each other, up there on the cedar bench, shadowy figures in the dense steam. Marusa moved away quickly and I followed … reached to swack her bare behind as she jumped down. I swung, hit air, lost balance, fell on the rocks. Sizzling flesh … Marusa's gasp.

I got up quickly, walked into the outer room. "I won't look," and stood whimpering, watching my cousin as her eyes looked down at my shoulder, my arm. I saw fear, saw her mouth contort, heard her cry.

"Ana, oh Anachka," she rocked back and forth, not touching me.

"How does it look?"

"Oh awful. What shall we do. We need mama."

And as I looked at her, wondering why she was berserk when it hardly hurt at all, a grinding bolt of pain hit me and spread throughout my body and I heard Marusa's screams, realized they were my own and that frightened me even more.

I was walking toward the house, towel draped around me. Through the pain, I saw that Marusa wasn't wearing a blouse. Just a towel thrown over her jeans. The towel had slipped and her breasts were showing and I tried to laugh, tell her old Teemonya would see and to cover herself, but then a black wave rolled over me and I slumped down on the path, and as I fell, I realized my towel had slipped off too.

Through a haze, I was aware of Marusa and Teemonya helping me up the stairs and into Marusa's bed, cool cloths being placed around the burn.

"Oh ... I wish we had a telephone."

"It doesn't look good, docha, she needs a doctor."

"But everyone's gone."

"You go tell babka. She's healed many burns."

"I'm afraid of her."

"They say she has the evil eye," I whispered, and no one heard.

"Ach ... it's not the time to be afraid. Go."

Marusa ran out, clattered down the wooden stairs. Old Teemonya kept shaking his head, looking down at me, his veined hands trembling. And then Marusa was in the room, saying they had to take me to the little house where all the medicines and roots were and the three of us started out down the long hallway, the staircase where we had to walk single file, and out into the blinding sunlight. I was no longer afraid of anything except dying. Did one die of a burn on one's arm and shoulder?

I was helped onto a cot, a cup at my lips. I choked, and swallowed something bitter. An incredibly wrinkled face looked down at me. Filmy grey eyes, white hair framed by a shawl tied under the chin, pouched mouth like the opening of an old paper bag.

"Don't hurt me with the evil eye," I said in Russian.

She looked down at me for a long minute, and I thought she smiled.

"We have no time for foolishness now. You and Teemonya go about your business," she said to Marusa, "But before you do, I'll need a little help preparing a poultice."

Marusa looked frightened. However, she fetched a basin, poured warm water. The old woman, back bent, her full skirt swaying, limped over to the cupboard and removed a small bag tied tightly with string. We watched her untie it, pour out a greenish powder, stir it into the water. She laid out a clean white cloth and spread the paste onto it and lifting it, put it against my burning shoulder. I yelled out as I felt the cold.

"Lie down. Rest."

"Ana, don't fall asleep. She gave you something to drink and it might put a curse on you." Marusa bent over, whispered in English. I hoped the bapka couldn't understand.

"Oh, I won't," I closed my eyes.

The old woman, Hanya, settled down beside the bed, watching the sleeping girl. The burn was a bad one, one of the worst she'd seen in her many days of being a lekarka. She hoped the poultice would work. She'd gathered the herbs fresh just two days before, so they should be potent. Hanya bent over the flushed face, wiped beads of sweat from the forehead, upper lip. She hoped the girl hadn't been so frightened that she'd develop a stutter, or a twitch when she healed. She had to make sure, rose, went to the cupboard, removed a small pair of scissors. Gently she took Ana's hand and looked at the short nails, shook her head. However, she managed to cut a tiny sliver without waking her. Next, she lifted a long strand of pale blonde hair and snipped off an inch or two. She removed a tiny piece of honeycomb wax from a jar, took the nail and hair in her hand, rolling the wax around it until it was a small soft ball.

Hanya stepped out onto her stoop, shuffled over to an old birch tree beside the house, dug inside a knothole with a knife. She inserted the ball into the hole and sealed it off neatly. Standing back, she whispered a molitva, a prayer, telling evil spirits not to be, not to dwell here, asking God to take their place, repeating the ancient words three times. The dirt path swam up and around, and she reached for the wooden porch railing, closing her eyes, listening to the chanting inside her head. Good spirits or bad? She'd been hearing them often lately. Hanya went inside and took up her vigil beside the girl.

She wasn't sure when she'd first realized she had the healing power. But ever since she was tiny, she'd been fascinated with the rows of jars and bags of powders near her baba's bed. Baba was her papa's mother and they lived together in the small house in the village in Russia. She accompanied her baba out into the fields, helping her pick the plants and dig the roots for the medicines, depositing them into her grandmother's apron. She remembered praying over her baby brother, helping her baba mix root teas, wiping his waxen body with cooling cloths, while her mother had moaned and rocked herself, snatching up the infant in relief when the fever finally left. She'd been just eight.

She remembered the time she'd been compelled to use her gift when she was a young woman with eyes the colour of rain and a long, light brown braid with tight, fuzzy curls escaping from it. There were hundreds of people gathered on a large mountain meadow, praying and singing around a burning pyre of guns. The singing and praying went on all night. Next morning they watched as a cloud of cossacks on horseback, the cavalry, approached, thundered through the crowd. Shouting, they cracked whips over the men who were standing in the front, calmly singing psalms, renouncing guns, vowing never to kill anyone. Faces split from eye to jaw, blood spurted. The praying went on. The stunned masses, many bleeding, were herded several kilometres back to the villages.

And it was then Hanya had helped her baba clean wounds, apply poultices, bandages, and they'd prayed. Because the special molitvi were just as important as the medicines. She discovered she wasn't sickened by the sight of blood, the gaping flesh. She felt needed.

And she'd been thankful that all children had been left at home that night.

The girl, "Ana" Marusa had called her, moaned and opened her eyes, saw Hanya sitting beside her. For an instant she looked startled, then she gave a small sigh and her body relaxed and she lay quietly while Hanya felt her forehead, cheeks, with her wrinkled brown hand. She was so hot. Hanya hoped she wouldn't get the fever. She pulled back the bandage, examined the flesh. A clear, yellowish fluid oozed from the burn, and the area around it was red with tiny blisters. There might be scarring, but not if she could help it. Young girls didn't cover their bodies like they did before. Ana would have trouble getting a husband.

The lightheaded feeling returned and Hanya groped for the chair, sank down again. Her old body was stiff, wanting to lie on her narrow bed, sink into the feather pereenah, pull the wool-filled quilt up to her chin. But she had to watch the girl, give her more of the bitter root tea to calm her if she awoke.

I opened my eyes, ran my tongue around cracked lips, tasting dryness. I saw the old woman sitting beside my cot. She was sleeping, head bent over her lap. It was quiet in the house, almost dark. I looked out the window and saw the sun setting behind the mountains. I'd slept all afternoon. Where was Marusa? I'd find her before the woman awoke. But I was so tired and my shoulder throbbed, and maybe if I just closed my eyes for a minute I'd feel better.

I was part of the crowd on the mountain. I was singing a hymn, my head covered with a platok, my skirt long. I saw the pile of guns being lit, tasted the bitter smoke as it rose in the night sky. I didn't see anyone I knew, yet I wasn't afraid. For this was familiar. Even the hymn was familiar and my voice rose and blended with the hundreds of voices. And then I knew what would happen next and felt afraid. All night the singing went on and my fear grew. I began to cry, to make my way to the back of the crowd, but I couldn't move. The people stood close together, singing and praying. No one looked at me ... no one felt my hands pushing at them, trying to part a path through the crowd. I shouted, "Go. Before it's too late," but no one listened. And then it was morning and in the distance, I heard the pounding of hooves and I screamed. But the singing went on and then it was too late.

The boat was a creaking rusty hulk, its hold packed with clothing, tents, everything the passengers owned in the entire world. Hanya remembered watching the lush greenness of Cyprus grow smaller. It had not been a kind land, the months in exile from Russia stealing many lives in the steamy heat. The sweet smell of death had hung over the villages day and night. Hanya had worked frantically with her grandmother and the other lekarkee trying to save people unused to the tropics. They often failed. And then Hanya's own baba had succumbed to the heat and the fever, been buried in the alien land, and as the ship ploughed out to sea, Hanya and the others said goodbye to loved ones cradled forever in foreign soil.

The second day at sea, Hanya saw the deckhand...his merry brown eyes, strong white teeth. She especially stared at the muscled bare chest. He saw her watching him and grinned and she quickly put her hand to her hair, tucking in wayward curls beneath her shawl, selfconscious. He was slopping dirty water around with a broom, winking when he caught her eye, reddening when a man shouted something at him. And she fell in love.

They didn't speak. Couldn't understand each other anyway. Yet they passed regularly on the deck, smiling, seeking each other's eyes. And finally there had been kisses behind the lifeboat when everyone was down below eating, or when the weather was rainy or stormy. They would brace themselves against the wall, secure behind the lifeboat, whisper in a language neither comprehended, understanding only the joy of holding each other despite the bulk of Hanya's clothing.

"Are you going to marry him in Canada ... leave the Doukhobors ... become Anglichka?" Nastya, her friend whispered. They were sitting on the deck in the sun, wind flipping their shawls, the hems of their skirts.

"How can I? I don't understand him when he speaks. Besides, my mother needs me to help with cooking."

"As if the cooking would stop me," said Nastya.

The room was dark, but I could see the old woman sitting beside my bed, head bent, hear the quick, shallow breaths. It was quiet in the night, the only sound the barking of a distant dog. And then I heard another sound, sort of a chant, and looked around for a radio. But it seemed to be coming from outside the house and I covered my head with the quilt. Was it the bapka's evil spirits begging to be let in? I wanted to get up, find Marusa, but was afraid.

And then I was following the shabby crowd off the creaking grain boat, tripping over my bundle. Why didn't anyone help? "Here, take this end, please." I'd asked nicely of the woman with the small boy. Why didn't she pick up one corner of the heavy blanket containing everything I owned and help me carry it? Couldn't she see how I stumbled along behind everyone? The crowd surged ahead, anxious to see their new home ... all except the young girl and the boy, the deckhand. They were standing off to the side, holding each other, faces wet. The girl broke away, followed the crowd without looking back. He stood unmoving until the doors of the huge immigration building swallowed her.

"You fool," I yelled. "Stay with him. You're going to ruin your body breaking prairie soil. You will crave rest while you dig seneca roots to make money for the community. You'll be better off being a sailor's wife, living in a little house near the harbour. And you will have your love."

The girl kept walking, didn't turn her head, and I picked up my heavy bundle, followed her inside, tripping over my long skirts.

The low hum of voices wakened Hanya. She listened for a long time, trying to hear the words. There were none. Just an eerie tuneless chant and again she tried to assess whether it was angels or devils. She eased her cramped body upwards, hanging onto the chair for support, made her way to the table, lit the coal oil lamp, bringing it over to the cot. Holding the lamp carefully, she pulled the quilt from the head of the girl, touched the sleeping face. Cooler now, the breathing light. She examined the burn, saw that the redness was gone. The skin was puckered around the edges, the injured area now had a thin film over it and was no longer weeping. The healing process had begun. There would be no scarring. The herbs and molitvi had done their job.

Hanya took off her shoes, lay down on her bed, pulled up the quilt over her shoulders. Remembered a long ago night when molitvi hadn't mattered. She and her husband, son and daughter had left the prairie lands they'd tilled. "Swear allegiance to the flag and country." "We cannot. God is our king ... we recognize Him only." And the homestead lands were taken and the people were on the move again, this time to the misty mountainous valleys of British Columbia. The days on the boat and the young deckhand were as if they'd never happened.

They'd been asleep in their cramped apartment in the village when voices exploded in the courtyard. Volodya had jumped up, pulled pants over his combination, run outdoors barefoot. Hanya paused, listening as the shouts became louder, intermingled with wailing, hastily pulled on skirt, blouse, fumbled for shoes under the bed and fearfully followed her husband into the dawning night.

"Our leader is dead."

"Train explosion in the mountains."

"Bomb in the coach."

Shock ... disbelief ... anger and sorrow. Who had done this unspeakable thing? And then the molitvi. At first to pray it wasn't so. That someone had misunderstood. Then prayers for the soul and eternal peace of the man they called "Lordly". And on an autumn day she joined the hundreds as they walked up the mountain to bury him and the music of their sorrowful singing echoed over the valley.

I was watching the pre-dawn sky through the window, waiting for the first slice of light when I'd steal away to the big brick house and carefully crawl into bed next to Marusa. The outline of a face appeared in the dark glass. My face with a platok tied around it, hair cut in bangs across my forehead, longsleeved blouse with tucks and lace. I was dozing, my body gently lurching, swaying with each bend the train turned. And there were many bends in these rugged mountains. I was thankful it was dark and I could not see how high we were, how far below were the narrow valleys. The conductor walked through the coach, but didn't speak to anyone. He'd already collected our tickets and it was late and everyone slept.

My eyes flew open. Escape. I had to get out. I looked around. The doors were locked, the only way out was at the ends of the coaches where they were hitched together. If I jumped, I'd likely roll down the mountain ... or worse, we'd be on a high bridge between the cliffs. I tried the window, pulled it down a little. Too tiny for my body. I half rose from my seat, sat down. Everyone was asleep, gently moving in rhythm to the clicks of the wheels. I was trapped. I felt sweat trickle between my breasts. The man on the seat across from me slept, his newspaper spread across his lap. The date on it said October 1924.

"We have to stop the train, get out."

I leaned across, rattled the paper, finally shook his arm. He continued to sleep.

"Mr. Conductor," I yelled in relief as I saw the uniform appear at the end of the coach, "Stop the train. We all have to get off ... hurry."

He kept walking down the aisle, looked at me, and through me. Why didn't he help? Why was he pretending I wasn't here?

And when the fear became so great, and I wanted to claw my way out the window, a mighty sound shook the coach, finally stopped the train. Lights swayed ... people smashed against each other ... too stunned to scream. The sound reverberated across the valley ... slammed into rugged mountains on the other side ... bounced from rock to massive rock in diminishing echos. Then, the most terrible sound of all ... silence. And ever so slowly, through the open window began the chatter of birds, the rustlings of frightened animals. Crunch of feet on cinder rocks ... shouts ... lanterns ... moans. I didn't have to get up ... go outside to look. I knew. Twisted steel ... seats ripped open. People thrown out into the cold night. Rag dolls. Limbs torn. Eyes staring into the black sky.

Hanya lay in her bed watching the dawn. She was so cold. Even the quilt couldn't make her old bones warm. And then she heard it again ... the chanting. Only this time there were words. A psalm her people had sung long ago while the corpses of their guns lay among the ashes. It was strange how singing was always present at the most important events. She had to get up ... see who was outside her window.

She pushed aside the quilt, put her feet on the floor. Never mind the shoes, she had stockings. She walked to the door and opened it. The singing grew louder. To her surprise, there was no one there. And then she saw a young man, really a boy. Not Volodya, for she'd never known him until he was older. She saw the brown eyes, the wide smile. Hanya smiled back and without hesitation followed him into the cold dawn.

I awoke to warm sunlight flooding the room through cobwebby curtains, the red geraniums glowing with color and wondered why I was so afraid yesterday. My burn was healing, the pain nearly gone and I was hungry.

I rose, looked across the room at the narrow bed where the old woman had been sleeping. I tiptoed over to the bed. She was still asleep, a smile on her face making her look almost youthful. I reached out and touched her hand, looked down at her for a moment, then walked out of the house and gently closed the door. I had to find Marusa and Teemonya, tell them the angels had come on the wings of the night.

Broken Branch

"Do your girls know, Katya? Ana is surely old enough."

Molly from across the field was at the kitchen table when I came in from school. Her husband had disappeared a long time ago and she had brought up her daughter Lily by weeding gardens. She spent a lot of time in our kitchen as if the chaos at our house provided some relief from her quiet, orderly and oppressive life.

I took off my heavy coat and the high rubbers which fit over my shoes. Soon the mud and dirty snow would be gone and we'd wear only shoes to school, feet wonderfully light. I pretended to be busy putting books away, but I was listening hard.

My mother and Molly talked about neighbours and relatives and their various illnesses and marriages and pregnancies in between exchanging recipes and the latest prices at the co-op. I'd be so quiet they'd forget I was there.

"I'll tell her when the time is right."

"Don't wait too long, Katya. You're showing already."

Mama looked over at me, made a shushing sound.

I put down the teacup I'd just filled and walked out of the kitchen and up the stairs to my bedroom. I sat on the edge of the bed, staring out the window at the snow swirling in big wet flakes.

So it's true, I kept thinking. I hadn't imagined it. My mother's swelling belly was a baby after all and not the result of too much food as I'd prayed. I'd even told her to exercise, saying the winter months were making her fat. Mama had smiled and I'd pushed the suspicion to the back of my mind.

But now I had to face it. My mother was going to have a baby. A fourth child. I was thirteen, already in high school and my parents were still having babies. I pictured the coming months. Visitors Day at school with my pregnant mother in attendance. My friends Zina and Marion asking pointed questions. Both of their mothers were old, didn't even sleep with their fathers. Zina's mother had gout, and Marion's father snored and besides Zina and Marion were change-of-life babies. Their mothers had both acquired a jowly, grandmotherly appearance and I couldn't imagine either of them having sex.

I'd always been extremely proud of my slender, brown-haired mother who was fun, spoke English fluently, even had been to grade eight back on the prairies. She liked to sit and talk with my friends, wanted to know about boys we liked at school and what the latest styles were.

She'd met my father shortly after her family moved to British Columbia to a small farm, and she'd joined the choir of young people. Prairie girl. Stylish. So different from the other girls who sang with her. They all wore their hair short with bangs, while she had long, curly hair, short skirts, blouses with big soft bows, spiky shoes. She caught the eye of the earnest young man in the row of tenors. They'd courted, part of a large group walking the dusty roads and dancing on the wooden bridge to accordian music, or rode in the Model A pickup truck crammed full of boys and girls singing Russian folk songs. She'd retained her sense of fun, despite the drudgery, and was less serious than my overworked father.

Now I wished she were more like my friends' mothers. Elderly and grey haired and rounded, speaking Russian only, not interested in my activities, just wanting to rest before the next group of grandchildren came to visit.

"Your mother's cheezsholaya, expecting, isn't she?" Marion said.

We'd been walking up and down Blackstone Avenue one late-spring evening. This promenade took place every Saturday night providing the weather was pleasant. It was a ritual everyone we knew participated in. Friends, relatives, and neighbours drove their pickup trucks or cars into town, parked in the co-op lot and bought their groceries, then proceeded to promenade up and down the two main streets, Oxford and Blackstone which met in a V on the corner right in front of the Stargate Café and Bus Depot. We formed chattering clusters, talking in both Russian and English, ignoring the Angleekee and the other inhabitants who had to make a wide circle around the laughing groups as they went about their business. They never joined in and were never asked to.

Women, some in kerchiefs, others like mama with freshly washed and curled hair, wore their prettiest summer outfits, starched and ironed. Men wore suspendered dress pants and white shirts rolled up at the sleeves. They wore shlapas, hats, usually with a tiny feather stuck jauntily in the headband, their sunburnt necks white where the hair had been cut just for the weekend. They sipped on bottles of Orange Crush, while children in their Sunday best played tag or begged their parents for a nickel, ran into the Stargate to emerge a minute later with a vanilla ice cream cone, a whip of licorice, or a box of Cracker Jack.

Zina and Marion and I would meet at the co-op, and after walking up and down in front of the Regal Theatre, past Murphy's Drugstore, the Tally-Ho Ice Cream Parlour and Coffee House, would go inside the Stargate Café, slide into an enamelled green booth, sip on a Grape Crush all evening, ignoring Mama Rose Wong, the Chinese owner, who always told us to move along if we weren't ordering food. The Stargate had the only jukebox in town, and was always packed.

It was the first time my friends had mentioned my mother's pregnancy. In fact it was the first time she'd worn the telltale maternity smock, and there was no mistaking what was underneath the loose flowered folds as she'd stepped down awkwardly off the truck. I saw Marion and Zina waiting for me on the sidewalk, so I positioned myself right in front of mama hoping I was hiding her large stomach. For weeks I'd been running outside to join my friends as soon as they appeared in our yard, not inviting them inside the house. Or if they did make it into the kitchen, I'd stand in front of my mother, hoping to hide her secret. Up until tonight, I had succeeded.

However, they didn't mention the smock as I ushered them down Blackstone Avenue and away from my mother, chattering about the kissing posters in front of the Regal Theatre.

But I should have remembered that Marion noticed everything and that she had a one track mind. I took a big gulp of Crush, swished it back and forth from cheek to cheek, carefully planned my answer.

"I haven't noticed anything, except how much she eats. She eats all the time. That's why she's so fat." I deliberately took a noisy slurp of pop, trying to distract them, hoping the subject was closed.

"It's just her stomach that's big, Ana. Her arms and legs are really skinny. She must be cheezsholaya." I knew I had to wait until Marion had her say. "I heard my mother telling the neighbours about it, wondering if your parents were trying for a son. I'm sure glad I have two older brothers and I don't have to worry about babies anymore. Besides, my parents are too old to do it."

"Mine are too old too," Zina said with pride. "Imagine that, Ana, your mother is still having babies and you're grown up. Almost."

Until now, Zina and Marion and I had shared everything. "Troika, padrooshki," we'd say, trio, girlfriends, as we walked from Zina's house to my house to Marion's house across the fields, sharing secrets. Now I felt separate from them.

Mama brought up the subject of the baby one day when we were alone in the living room, folding clothes I'd pulled off the clothesline.

"These need darning," she said, adding another pair of socks to the growing pile. "I swear you girls are worse than your father," and without warning, "You know there's going to be a baby, don't you?"

I didn't look up from the tea towels I was folding. "Yeah. I noticed. So have my friends."

"And you're upset about it?"

"I'm too old to have a baby brother or sister. None of my friends have babies at home. It's so embarrassing.

How come you decided to have one anyway?"

"We wanted to try one more time for a boy. You know, once you girls are married, the Katelnikoff name will be gone. At least this branch will be."

"I can keep my name forever."

"Not if you get married. You know a woman always takes her husband's name. Oh, I sure hope it's a boy. Mostly for your father's sake. He'd teach him to drive the truck, take him everywhere. They'd be pals. I'd like a little boy too." She smiled as if she already visualized him.

"He'd be a spoiled little brat," I said and gave the sheets a vicious jerk. Why couldn't my father teach me to drive, and be my pal.

Sometimes I didn't understand my mother. She'd act fun and silly, learning the newest jive steps with us, then become serious and wifely when my father's truck drove into the yard. And now she was all worried about producing an heir for the Katelnikoff family. As if it were her ultimate goal in life and nothing else mattered. Was it to please my father who was a fine singer and speaker at the sobranye, when she didn't care for the formality and ceremonies? Perhaps she felt guilty? She would rather visit with friends over a cup of tea, taking her brood with her, or meet the new neighbours, even if they were Angleekee?

That night as I lay in bed, I imagined my brother's face in the darkness. Saw the rounded cheeks of the child become the highly planed cheekbones of the adult. Blonde hair, brown eyes. The brown eyes possibly a throwback to some long ago ancestor who was tall and straight, kind and sensitive, cape thrown over his shoulders as he rode his horse across the Russian steppes. My brother would inherit all of these romantic qualities and be a basketball star besides.

I didn't stop to ponder how any one person could possibly possess all these admirable attributes. I only knew that if the baby were a boy, he would be exceptional, and I'd know it immediately, and suddenly I was excited.

My mother wanted to name him Kondrat after my father, so I decided I'd call him Ken. He'd tease me, call me "sis" as he sat at the kitchen table devouring the cookies I'd baked just for him.

I told Sara and Lisa about our brother.

"But I want a sister," Lisa whined. She wasn't happy about being replaced as the baby.

"You're crazy. We already have three girls. Papa wants a son."

"But I don't have a baby sister."

"We're having a brother," Sara said with firmness. And that was that, for no one argued with Sara.

I began asking my mother if she was drinking lots of milk, getting her exercise, as recommended in her "Canadian Mother and Child Manual".

The days got warmer and my mother's girth increased.

One day when I visited my grandparents at the farm, and I was helping deda clean out the barn, he brought up the subject of the baby. I was a little embarrassed, concentrated on spreading fresh straw on the floor. We didn't talk about such things to fathers and grandfathers.

"Docha," he said in the gentle way he talked to all of us grandchildren, "You will be having a little one in the house soon, and God willing it will be healthy. For the family it would be wonderful to have a son because the name will not die out. Your aunts have boys but they're not Katelnikoffs. Only your father's children can have the name, and someday, when he and I are both gone, and if there is no son, this branch of the family tree will be broken forever. But with a boy, the branch will spread and grow and the tree will be strong."

I asked baba if she thought sons were better than daughters.

"No, not better, but everybody wants a sinochik," she said in Russian, her quick brown fingers snapping beans, putting them into canning jars. "That way the family name carries on. We prayed you'd be a boy, but it didn't turn out that way and with each baby we got more worried that it wouldn't happen. When the bapka took you and your sisters out of your mother and picked you up, your other babushka and I were there, and we held our breath, waiting for her words. And every time she said, 'dochichka'. Fine and healthy, but a daughter. And though we loved each of you, in our hearts we prayed for an oonook. But this time it will be different. I can feel it. Besides, I held the needle over your mother's stomach, and the needle moved and danced around on the thread, so I knew it was a boy. If the needle hangs straight and still, it's a girl. It was that way with all of you." She nodded her head in satisfaction. "This time it's a Katelnikoff grandson."

It was incredible that so much hope rested on the tiny, kicking, growing human in my mother's stomach. He wasn't even born, yet already he was destined to be heir apparent to the family name, my father's future companion, the pride of my grandparents.

Mama made monthly visits to Dr. Tenholme who said she was a bit anaemic but otherwise healthy. He told her to eat red meat, and she told him she was brought up vegetarian and would eat lots of eggs and milk instead. She'd get lots sicker if meat ever touched her lips.

She was planning to go into the hospital to give birth this time. When she'd had Sara and Lisa and me, papa had gone and brought the bapka, midwife, to the house, along with our babas, and we were born right in the double bed.

"Ana was the hardest, but you two were quick. Only took three hours. This one will be fast too, I know it. But then boys might be different."

She was folding our old baby clothes, freshly washed and ironed, and I noticed a soft new blue blanket among the pink and white garments. She placed it inside the crib we'd all slept in. My father had brought it down from the attic, sanded it, painted it blue and white.

One day when I was in the co-op, in the notions section, I spotted baby books. The kind where you write in details about the baby, like weight and colour of hair and eyes and lists of gifts. I chose one with a blue cover and a family tree inside, just like deda had said, with branches where you filled in the names of grandparents, parents, brothers and sisters. At the top of the tree was a little twig, my baby brother. I bought the book and hid it in my room, filled in all our names and at the top I lightly printed in pencil "Ken (Kondrat)."

We discussed what we'd do when the pains began. If it were night or a weekend, papa would drive mama to the hospital and I'd look after my sisters. If he was at work, I'd run across the newly harvested field of oats, skirt the alfalfa and go straight up the hill to the Lymans and get them to come and drive my mother to the hospital. They were the nearest neighbours with a vehicle. Everyone else around us either walked or rode a bicycle.

I was hoping I wouldn't have to go for the Lymans, because last year in a frenzy of midsummer madness and a delighted daring, my sisters, led by me, had trampled Mr. Lyman's field of lush, green-black alfalfa. It had looked so pristine, straight and tall, ready for harvest that hot summer evening, that a strange joy had overcome me and I'd taken a tentative step into its green coolness, and was lost. I ran barefoot across the field, circling, shouting to my sisters to join me. Sara and Lisa, after the first shocked gasps, followed, zig-zagging, laughing, until we stood exhausted and silent, staring at the devastated field.

Someone had seen us performing our wild dance and early the next morning, even before our father had left for work, Mr. Lyman stomped down the hill, the empty sleeve of his left arm quivering as he stabbed the air with his other hand and shouted. My father, appalled, had lined us up in a row and made us say, "how sorry we are, Mr. Lyman. We'll never do it again" in soft, sobby voices.

"Ana will pay you out of her babysitting money." And subdued and chastened, I made the weekly pilgrimage up the hill each Sunday afternoon after sobranye with the fifty cents I earned babysitting Mrs. Nichvolodoff's terrible twin boys Saturday nights. It had taken me forty weeks to pay off that one mad, delicious moment. And the farmer who rented the field from Mr. Lyman had to go elsewhere for his hay that summer.

The Lymans, Chesterfield and Clara, arrived in our valley right after the war, following their war bride daughter to Canada. The daughter had long since left her husband and returned to England, but the Lymans were too old to follow, existing in their large, lonely, untidy house with generations of the royal family staring haughtily from every wall. They drove their ancient green Packard slowly and jerkily to town and back, Mrs. Lyman having to shift the gears because of Mr. Lyman's having only one arm. He'd lost his left arm in the First World War, and I can only wonder what they thought when they found themselves living among a group of pacifists who didn't believe in wars or killing of any kind.

It was also Mrs. Lyman's job to honk the horn and she did so every few yards, scattering dogs and children, and we were thankful she didn't drive, as her eyesight was terrible.

So the last thing I wanted to do was ask the Lymans to take my mother to the hospital and I prayed the baby would decide to come when my father was home. My father was working overtime all that summer, carpentering at the sawmill, coming home well after dark, eating the supper left on the edge of the still warm cookstove.

One sticky evening in late August, after a whole week of canning fruit and vegetables, storing the jars in the root cellar under the house, we were scrubbing floors and counters.

Mama was washing the floor when she said "oh" in a surprised sort of way, put down the mop and walked into her bedroom, shutting the door.

I kept thinking that it couldn't be the baby — it was much too soon — and continued polishing the black cooking surface of the stove. Sara and Lisa hadn't noticed anything, just kept on squabbling at each other across the dishwater.

I pushed at the door, saw my mother sitting on the bed, cupping her stomach with her hands as if to keep the baby there for a while longer. A last act of protection.

"Is it the baby? Is it being born now?"

My sisters pushed me into the room, both quiet for a change.

"My water broke and I don't think I should wait for your father. Ana, you run and get the Lymans and you two help me get dressed. Sara, you get the suitcase out of the closet. The little brown one. It's already packed. Get going, Ana, your brother isn't going to wait. Oh, and stop in at Molly's. Tell her to come right over. Hurry." She ended on a little gasp.

I flew out the door, barefoot, across the newly mown field of oats, not even noticing the sharpness on my feet. I felt the inky darkness, soft and thick and black on my bare arms and legs, my face. The night air smelled of hay and wild clover and I could hear the songs of the frogs and crickets as I ran.

Molly's lamp shone orangely in her kitchen window. I pounded on the door, hollering at her to open it and come help my mother.

"Och nyanichka. Nada lekarstva." My goodness. I bring medicines and herbs. When Molly was agitated, she always spoke in Russian.

"No, you don't understand. She's going to the hospital this time. The Lymans will take her. You stay with her until we come."

"Lymans not too quick. They'll take long time getting there. She'll need medicine."

Molly put her shoes on as she muttered about the Lymans, mooh davyoot, squashing flies, they moved so slow, she said, while she got a small bundle out of the cupboard, blew out the lamp and followed me outside, starting back across the stubbly oat field with her limping rheumatic gait.

I ran alongside the alfalfa field, my legs becoming entangled in the tall grass. Through the damp patch where my feet sank in cold, soft mud. Hurry. Up the hill and through the yard. Up the porch steps. No lights. Wait. There, in the back bedroom, a light burned. I knocked. Banged some more. What if they refused to help. We didn't say much when I handed them my weekly payments. Just a polite "here's the money" and "thank you." Maybe they were still angry with me and my whole family.

Then I saw lights flare in the kitchen. The door finally opened to reveal Mrs. Lyman in flannel and hairnet, Mr. Lyman in a long combination, his sparse hair standing out in white wisps. Mrs. Lyman fumbled with her glasses, put them on and peered at me.

"What are you doing here at this hour?"

"It's only nine o'clock." I defended myself. Then the words came in a great rush. "My mother's baby is coming. Can you come and get her. Take her to the hospital. My father's not home."

"Oh my, oh my ..." Visibly agitated, Mrs. Lyman opened and closed her mouth several times, "Chesterfield, we have to get dressed."

"There's no time. Just come now. Please."

Mr. Lyman darted about in confusion, finally got his keys, and to my relief they put coats over their shoulders and followed me into the night.

We drove into our yard and I ran into the house, while the Lymans bustled about, opening all the car doors, and leaving the headlights on. Sara and Lisa huddled on the sofa, looking scared.

"How is she?"

"I don't know. Molly's in there."

"She said to stay out and be quiet. Oh Ana, will

mama be all right?"

"Of course. She's had babies before."

"But Molly said it will be a surprise if the baby waits for the hospital."

"Don't make up stories, Lisa."

"She did, she did say it."

I slowly opened the bedroom door, afraid to go in.

"Noo ... you took your time," Molly said to me.

I looked at my mother's white face, at her hands gripping Molly's so tight the knuckles stood out.

"Go tell the Lymans to get the doctor," Molly said. Then turning back to mama she motioned toward her bundle. "You want something for pain?"

"No. I don't want to get sleepy."

"But the hospital," I said, "Aren't you going?"

"No time." My mother's voice, sounding strained and high.

"Tell them to hurry and then you come right back. I need you to help get this baby borned." I'd never heard Molly sound officious before. "Behee skaray," she added. Run, hurry.

I went out, sent the Lymans for Dr. Tenholme, begging them to drive as fast as they could, then went back into the bedroom with its grotesque shadowy walls, the writhing figure on the bed, smells of sweat and hope.

"Wash your hands, Ana, then help me. The head is already coming. It won't be long." Molly bent over the bed, "And get me basin with warm water and towels and scissors."

I finally looked down at my mother's face and she smiled through her pain and said "Guess you'll be helping bring your brother or sister into the world," and I began trembling and couldn't stop.

I came back from the kitchen and watched with

fascination and revulsion as my mother pushed and groaned and I vowed I'd never have a baby. Molly finally guided the slimy little creature out into the world and I heard it give a lusty cry.

Molly took the scissors, bent over the bed, hiding the baby from my view. Mama half sat, watching her.

"That looks fine," she said. "That's a good job."

Then Molly wrapped the baby in the little blue blanket, said "devochka", little girl, and laid her in mama's arms.

I stood there in the stifling room, with the downy, newborn scent of my sister, feeling the scalding disappointment welling up in my throat, leaving a bitter taste.

"Come look, Ana. She's beautiful."

I stared at mama. How could she be so happy, the longed-for son already forgotten?

"Do you want to hold her?"

I looked down at the wizened red face in the crook of her arm. A stranger in the place of my brother.

"She was supposed to be a boy. What will papa say?"

I ran out of the room, past Sara and Lisa, yelling "It's another girl" as I went outside.

I wandered around the yard, watching for truck lights, dreading first the anticipation, then the disappointment, on my father's face. It was all my mother's fault. She was the one who had the baby, told us it would be a boy.

Now there were four girls. Women everywhere. Houseful of high, shrill voices, screams, giggles. No boyish shouts, deep laughter except for our father. No toy cars and wagons, miniature carpenter tools, hockey sticks. Just more pink hair ribbons, paperdoll books, frilly underwear. More dolls with eyes that opened and closed and who ridiculously wet when you fed them water. Girls' toys filling our already crowded house.

A feeling of grief overcame me and I cried deep gulping sobs. It was as if my brother had died. As if I'd known him as a baby and a man, and now he was gone.

First thing in the morning, I'd get out the blue baby book, throw it into the woodstove, watch it burn.

I saw Dr. Tenholme's big car drive into the yard, soon followed by the Lymans. Grinding of gears. Shuddering stop. Then stillness, except for the drowsy nighttime sounds of the chickens and the frog chorus.

Finally the lights of our truck swept over the trees and the yard. I crouched, ran into a corner of the garden and sat down in a miserable huddle.

The truck door slammed shut. Quick footsteps on the porch. Door opening and closing. I covered my ears with my hands, shut my eyes tightly. Now he was walking through the kitchen into the bedroom. Seeing the baby and mother. I pressed my hands tighter until my ears rang. He now knew.

I saw the doctor's car leave, and realized I was shaking with cold, my limbs cramped. I got up and made my way toward the house.

The door opened and the Lymans walked onto the porch.

"We saw the baby," Mrs. Lyman said. "Such a pretty little girl."

"Strong fingers." Mr. Lyman chuckled.

"We had to come back and make sure your mother was fine. I'm glad we did, because we saw the little one. Like a rose, isn't she, Ducky?"

"Yes, a real beauty. Like our girl was. Remember? Now she has her own children in England and we've never seen them."

"We will if we save up enough alfalfa money. Send it to them for airplane tickets."

They carefully made their way down the steps in the darkness. Mrs. Lyman groped for the door handle, climbed in, gathered her long flannel nightgown after her.

"So many of you. So lucky," I thought she said, as the door clicked shut.

The house was quiet, the bedroom door closed. I went upstairs, saw the dim outlines of Sara and Lisa in their room, undressed in the dark and crawled into bed, slept deeply without dreaming.

"Mama says to get up right now," Lisa bounced on my bed, fully dressed. She was chewing on a piece of toast, smears of gooseberry jam around her mouth.

"I held my baby sister." Her eyes sparkled. She smiled happily. "I wanted a sister and I got one."

"You're the only one who did," I said in a grumpy voice. "Is papa at work?"

"No, he's going to get our babas first. Both of them. Because mama has to rest for one whole week."

I dressed slowly, made my way downstairs. My father sat in the kitchen, holding the blue bundle, talking baby talk.

"Well," he looked up at me, "What do you think of her? Isn't she pretty?"

"Yeah, I guess so."

"You did a lot last night. Going for the Lymans and helping Molly."

"That's okay," I shrugged, looked down at the pink face, unfocused eyes, the tightly clenched fists. "She's cute," I admitted.

We watched her for a minute.

"Don't you wish ... I mean, if it were a boy, wouldn't

you be just so happy?"

"Oh sure. But we have a healthy daughter."

Then he looked up and just for a moment I saw the pain in his eyes, and he said ever so softly so mama wouldn't hear, "Och Anachka, if it were a boy, this whole family would have had the biggest celebration it's ever seen."

That was the only time my father said anything about the son he'd never have. The only time.

Although sometimes when my aunts came to visit and brought their little boys, I'd catch the longing in his eyes as he looked at his nephews tumbling about. Only for a moment. And then his arms would tighten around Baby Elena, or he'd stroke Lisa's hair. As if to remind himself of what he did have.

The First of May

We were sitting in the shade behind the woodshed, which doubled as a summer kitchen, eating yellow cake with its thin white icing and silver sprinkles. It was a hot afternoon in late August and there were four of us — Julia Podrowski, my younger sisters Sara and Lisa, and me.

It was the very first time I'd met Julia. She and her mother had arrived at our front door that afternoon and our mothers hadn't stopped talking for the last couple of hours, telling us to go out and play. It seems they'd been friends in Saskatchewan before either had married. They had gone to dances at White Sands School and to the softball games and sobranye, even though Julia's mother, Ann, was an Independent Doukhobor, her family leaving the big group and buying their own farm, unlike mama's family who farmed the community lands.

Mr. Podrowski had worked as a bookkeeper on the prairies and decided to try the kinder climate of British Columbia, so he got a job in the accounting department at City Hall.

Mrs. Podrowski said she just couldn't wait to see her old girlfriend Katya, and even though it was Sunday, she'd taken a chance mama'd be home, and walked all the way from their house in town with Julia.

I'd never seen my overworked, responsible mother so giddy. She kept calling Mrs. Podrowski "Blondie". "Gee whiz, remember those songs we sang, Blondie." And they both began to sing:

When I shall quit my mortal shore
And mosey 'round the earth no more
Don't weep for me, don't cry, don't sob
I may have struck a better job.

"Oh God, remember the Friday afternoon dance classes at the back of the room? We always danced together because the boys never asked us," said mama.

"Except for Joe Siminoff. Remember he rode his horse to school and he had a big crush on you, but you wouldn't dance with him because you said he smelled like his horse," Mrs. Podrowski said, her eyes sparkly with laughter.

"Oh, Ann, the worst thing of all was that outhouse in winter. All frozen over so you couldn't sit. Everyone in the class knew where you had to go when you put your hand up."

Mama grabbed Mrs. Podrowski around the waist and they began to move in a slow waltz around our tiny living room.

Don't go and buy a large bouquet
For which you'll find it hard to pay
If you have roses, bless your soul
Just pin one in your buttonhole.

They ended in triumphant two-part harmony. Bowed low, then curtsied.

"Ann, do you remember Mr. Fairbrother? He made us sing that song every single Friday afternoon while we waltzed to it. And he was fresh too, always asking the grade eight girls to dance. Wonder what happened to him?"

"How about that Ukrainian boy, Harry Semchuk? Hubba Hubba Harry all the girls called him. He played 'Red River Valley' on his harmonica so sad it could make you cry. Katya, did you know that he followed me around the schoolyard and all the way home for a week, playing that tune until I told Mr. Fairbrother to make him stop?"

My mother saw all of us staring at her and Mrs. Podrowski, wiped her eyes and said, "Go — go out to play."

I tried not to stare at Julia who was the whitest, palest girl I'd ever seen. My sister Lisa and I were fair with freckles dusting our noses, and complexions which tanned gold in summer, and Sara had a nut brown look to her skin. But Julia had remained truly white that hot summer. Her face and thin arms were stained a faint pink, from the sun or from embarrassment, I couldn't tell which, and her long straight hair looked like pure spun gold. Pale lashes framed startlingly blue eyes which squinted behind gold-rimmed glasses. Blue veins pulsed under the translucent skin of her temples and on the insides of her long, thin wrists.

Julia was perched on a stack of boards, modestly holding the flared skirts of her blue sundress around her knees. It had no sleeves, just big ruffles over the shoulders. Imagine having a dress just for summer, one you didn't have to wear to school a whole season before passing down to your sisters.

I looked down at Julia's white socks and sandals and marvelled at how clean they were after her long walk on the dusty roads. She looked down at our bare brown feet, our navy shorts and stained t-shirts, then politely looked away.

"Want more cake?" I said with a touch of defiance. Just let her say something about our dusty, end of summer appearance, our rumpled untidy house. I'd heard her mother describe their nice little white house behind the school, with the tall maples and big lawn. There was just Julia and her parents, so their house would be neat and cool.

"I'd like some more, please. It's very nice cake. Did you make it?"

"I helped."

"Tell me about the grade six teachers."

I relaxed. Maybe we could be friends after all.

When school started, I took Julia around and showed her the playground, the ball field.

"I hate softball," she said.

"So do I. I'm afraid of the ball hitting me."

I was always last pick when we chose teams. I'd also set a record for most strikeouts.

"Here are the swings and teeters."

I pointed out all the nicest places to sit on the lawns underneath the maples, or on the cement staircases on the girls' side.

I took her down to the huge, dim basement in the bowels of the school, with its noisy, often-flooding toilets, its smells of stale peanut butter sandwiches and orange peels, showed her the huge cemented area where we played tag and "London Bridge" on cold days, girls on one side, boys on the other with a partition between. We never ventured to the boys' side where someone was always fighting, resulting in bloody noses and torn clothing, and where serious games of marbles were being played. The few show-off boys who sneaked over to the girls' side got tattled on, then publicly strapped.

That winter, our mothers didn't visit, as it was a long, snowy walk to our house, but at school, Julia and I were inseparable. We looked for each other first thing in the morning, borrowed each other's cardigans and hair barrettes and whispered a certain boy's name. "Promise you won't tell. Cross your heart and hope to die. Cross it."

Julia's father was Polish, so her last name ended differently from mine, and she lived in a pretty house. This made her acceptable to the other kids in town, and I was in fear she'd find a best friend from her neighbourhood. However, she remained true to me. Perhaps it was because of our mothers' friendship, or her mother also being Doukhobor.

We were partners as we walked to the auditorium to watch films ... "The British Columbia Department of Education presents 'The Stomach'."

"Ugh ... I'll never eat lunch again."

"Did you see those gastric juices boiling around, and what were all those shiny, ropy parts?"

We sat together and sang to the CBC Radio's School Music program Wednesday afternoons, and marched to assembly side by side and sang "Oh Canada", and listened to Mr. Cusick, the principal, speak about clean schoolyards and fighting in the boys' washroom, sunflower seeds on the oiled wooden floors, and speaking Russian on school grounds.

We borrowed each other's Pink Pearl erasers and new hexagon crayons and exchanged Valentines. I'd never had a best friend for such a long time.

"When we get married, we'll live in a duplex, side by side," we promised.

Julia had read about duplexes in her mother's *True Confessions* magazines. She'd also read, secretly, about love and passion and kissing, and we discussed all three in great detail. We wondered what the difference was between love and passion and planned the number of children we'd have.

"Only one ... a boy," I said, thinking of our cramped house and younger sisters.

"Two girls and two boys," said only-child Julia.

"I'll babysit," I offered generously.

And then April arrived, an April so beautiful with early blossoms and sunny days, we shed our heavy winter coats and rubber boots, and came to school in flowered cotton dresses and knee socks, even ankle socks, it was so warm.

The windows were open to catch the spring breezes and we could hear Mr. Lawrence's hand lawnmower and smell the freshly cut grass.

Mrs. Carstairs, our teacher, adjusted her elegant, dove-grey dress and patted her silver curls.

"Class, today we'll try out for the Maypole Dance."

A roar interrupted her, the boys groaning and the girls shrieking in great excitement.

"Silence!" The teacher's pale powdered cheeks turned pink. The colour rose up to her forehead and disappeared into her curls, a process which never failed to fascinate me.

Maypole dancing was just one part of the big May-day celebrations held each spring, an event based on an old-fashioned English springtime festival.

It included a May Queen who we all voted for, and her entire court, all from eighth grade. The Queen wore a purple velvet robe over her long white gown and her four maids of honour were in hooped organdy gowns of pink, lavender, green and yellow with matching bonnets. Tiny page boys carried the queen's train and little ringletted flower girls all in white with garlands of flowers encircling their foreheads, scattered petals and tried to stay in step. These were always the smallest, daintiest girls in second grade. I'd never been a flower girl.

The queen's escort was chosen by the teachers.

"You," they'd point to a tall, good-looking boy, "Let's see you walk. Straighten up now."

And often a quiet, nondescript boy would be transformed on Mayday into a handsome heart-throb in an unfamiliar suit, and consequently have his social life assured for the remainder of his school days.

The queen's court was preceded by a group of guards who marched into the grounds in their red uniforms and tall black hats, wooden rifles on their shoulders. None of the Doukhobor boys accepted the role of guard. Their parents would not approve.

The rest of the school took part in the pageant, with costumed dances being the most popular. I was usually a sunflower, not my favourite choice, considering the reputation sunflowers had in our school.

"Why can't I be a rose, or a bluebell. Their hats are so pretty."

"Never mind, Ana," my mother would always say, "when you're in sixth grade, you'll be in the Maypole Dance. That's my favourite. It's what Mayday is all about."

My friends and I dreamed of dancing the Maypole Dance, holding the long red and blue streamers attached to the top of a tall white pole, weaving the ribbons in an intricate pattern as we hippity-hopped in tandem with our partners.

Twelve boys and twelve girls were chosen for each of the two poles, dancing singly, then in pairs.

Being in the Queen's Court was an unattainable dream, but dancing the Maypole, dressed in ruffled white organdy, was something I'd looked forward to for years.

There were three sixth grade classes in our school, and we all practised for the tryouts, boys reluctantly and out of step, girls with great enthusiasm. Some even wore their best dresses and flared and twirled to show the teachers how pretty they'd look.

"I won't dance unless you're chosen too," I'd say to Julia.

"Neither will I."

Final tryout day arrived, and we all assembled on the lawn beside the freshly painted poles. The scratchy gramaphone groaned out the Maypole Dance and we picked up the ribbons and began hopping, linking arms with our partners. I was paired with Herby Moore, a squirming, noisy dervish who barely cleared my shoulder. I hunched down, ignoring Herby's clowning. We shuffled, tripped and hopped for the next few minutes. The teachers began calling names, cutting out the unsuccessful dancers.

"Ana and Herby," was one of the first called and we stepped out.

It was over. Now I would never dance the Maypole. Never hold the bright ribbon and skip around the pole in an intricate pattern. Never see my mother's proud smile as she pointed me out to her friends.

"Good," said Herby, "Now I don't have to dance that stupid dance."

I waited for Julia's name to be called. It never was. The music stopped and I waited for her to join me. But she continued holding onto the ribbon, laughing and talking. Had she forgotten our pact ... both or nothing?

She didn't look at me when I left.

The theme this year was "Seasons" and I was picked to dance in May. I was chosen to be a sunflower.

"You're nice and tall, Ana. It would look funny to have you a buttercup," Mrs. Carstairs said, patting her hair.

The music for our dance was an English country song with a sweet, haunting melody and we sang it as we did the dishes or fed the chickens.

Today's the first of May
Goodbye, goodbye dear friend.
We'll meet again someday, someday
We'll meet again someday
Before the first of May.

Even mama sang it as she sewed our costumes, or made her golden-brown blintsi for Sunday breakfast.

Julia and I still sat together in class, but we spent recess practising and didn't speak unless we had to. I was furious she didn't honour her promise and even angrier she didn't seem upset I wasn't chosen. Her success had driven an invisible wedge between us.

The days were sunny and warm. The old maples spread their huge branches over the lawns where we held our daily practises and everyone in town who had lilacs, roses or tulips promised to donate them for the great day.

I was both envious and resentful of Julia as I watched her dancing arm in arm with Andrew Rezansoff and I'd pretend I wasn't looking.

Mayday morning dawned and I was up early, padding around the house in bare feet, peering out at the pink and turquoise sky with relief. Dew sparkled on the tall grass surrounding the garden, and on the lilacs with their fine coating of dust.

I'd washed my long hair the night before and mama had rolled it into rag rollers and laid out our clothes on the chesterfield.

A few hours later, Sara and I were on our way to the schoolyard, where the Rhythm Band was sawing away in the front courtyard, under the tall flagpole with its Union Jack, and where small children were being lined up by harried teachers.

I saw Julia and the group of Maypole Dancers walk past and I looked away, pretending not to notice, hiding my envy. She was wearing a white organdy dress with four tiers of ruffles, and brand-new white patent leather baby doll shoes, the latest rage, and long white socks. I hoped she didn't see my plain white cotton with its deep hem and my newly-polished old shoes. It had taken three coats of white polish to cover the scuffs and we had bleached the laces and the socks. My hair looked nice though, with its unfamiliar curls and I swung it sideways as I talked.

The pageant unfolded as it always did. The flower girls were out of step and the queen stumbled twice during her speech. The public address system crackled as the mayor opened the festivities and proclaimed the thirty-third annual Mayday a civic holiday.

Our presentation was flawless for a change, and I smirked as the Maypole dancers made several mistakes, stopping to untangle the mess.

After the pageant mama came up to me, holding her Brownie Hawkeye Camera. "Ana, stand beside your sisters. And here's Julia. Here, put your arms around each other. Smile, both of you."

I moved reluctantly toward Julia and we stood stiffly, looking at the camera, then looked at each other and giggled and put our arms around each other self-consciously, as mama clicked.

Julia ran off, but from her smile, I knew she was ready to be friends, and I was too. However, I felt she should make the first move. After all, she'd broken her part of the bargain. It never occurred to ask myself what I'd have done in her place.

When I saw Julia on Monday, I allowed her the small polite smile I'd practised in front of my mirror all day Sunday.

"Tomorrow, I'll say 'good morning, Julia'. Maybe tomorrow," I said to Sara as we walked home in the warm afternoon, the scent of wild roses in the air. Sara didn't answer. She was humming "The First of May" as usual, and I joined in.

Julia's desk was empty next day. Then on Wednesday, Mrs. Carstairs paused at my desk.

"Ana, Julia is not feeling well. Perhaps you could drop off her homework at her house after school."

Mrs. Podrowski opened the door and led me through the neat living room with its photographs and doilies and waxed flower arrangements and lemon oil smell, and into Julia's little bedroom. I'd visited there a few times and envied Julia's pretty pink chenille spread, the dolls lined up on the chair and the games and books neatly stacked on the shelves.

Julia lay against the pillows, looking paler than ever in her white nighty. She raised her hand and fluttered it at me.

"Hi Ana."

"Hi. Are you feeling sick?"

"Yeah. Dr. Tenholme says it's a bad case of the flu. My legs and back ache and I have a fever, 101 degrees the doctor said." She sounded important, almost proud of the severity of her illness.

"That's awfully high, isn't it?" I had the desired reaction.

"Yes, very high. And I have to take some horrible medicine and my mother rubs my legs and back because my muscles are so stiff."

"I brought your homework. But I can always tell Mrs. Carstairs you're too sick to do it."

"No, I can do it, I guess. Ugh ... I don't want to. Are you still mad at me now that I'm so sick?"

"A little bit." I shrugged and stared at the sprinkler through the lacy curtain.

"Well ... you'd have probably done the same thing, you know. Danced the Maypole Dance."

"Not after I promised."

"Yes, you would."

"I don't know. Maybe."

"Do you still sing 'The First of May'?"

"Sometimes. Sara's always singing it. She drives me crazy."

"It's been going round and round in my head. I just love it. I sure wish it would've been our song for the Maypole Dance."

She began to sing and I joined in enthusiastically. "We'll meet again someday, someday. Before the first of May."

"Girls, girls," Julia's mother hurried in, "Ana, you'll have to go now. Julia needs her rest. Thank you for bringing her books."

I followed her out of the room and turned to wave at Julia.

"See you in my dreams, Julia," I said. It had been our special way of saying goodbye before the Maypole dance had come between us.

"I'll see you in mine first." She lifted a white hand in

farewell, then shut her blue-lidded eyes.

When I got home on Friday, mama said, "Julia's taken a turn for the worse. She's in hospital. I saw her mother in town today and she said Dr. Tenholme thinks it might be polio."

"Polio." I repeated the dreaded word. "But people die from polio."

"Sometimes they do. Julia's mother thinks it's probably all those popsicles you kids ate at May Day. They were much too cold. I told you to rest, not get too hot. You should never have visited her. Do you feel sick at all?" Her voice was sharp, the words coming out quick and loud. She was making vareniki for supper and her hands shook as she sealed the dough.

"No, I feel okay."

She put the plump pastries into a pot of boiling water then began chopping onions, loud thumping chops as if she were angry.

"Is Julia going to die? Will she be paralyzed?"

"No, no. But I want you girls to rest a lot and stay out of the sun. And I want you to watch your sisters because you're the oldest. Don't let them run around."

I spent a restless night, alternating between dreams and wakefulness and by morning I'd made up my mind to visit Julia. I'd have to make sure she knew I wasn't angry with her, that we were still friends. What if she died and I hadn't told her I'd forgiven her?

I told my mother I was going to town on my bike to buy a bottle of ink.

"Remember, don't get tired. And don't buy any ice cream or popsicles or cold pop. If you want a treat, get some licorice or peanuts." And for the third time already that day, she felt my forehead for fever.

I left my bike beside the walk leading to the old

cottage hospital and went up the steps. I opened the door, looked down the dark corridor, and reeled from the smell of Lysol and illness.

No one was around and I tiptoed quickly, trying to walk quietly on the shiny old linoleum. Past a door that said "Operating Room" and toward the back where the rooms were numbered. I couldn't see any nurses, just patients in white gowns who stared at me as I timidly poked my head in and out of the dim rooms.

In a small room, right at the very end, I came to a door which said "Isolation. No Visitors". I carefully pushed at it and looked inside. Julia lay on the bed, a large plastic tent over her, a machine on the table making an odd hissing sound. One end of a tube was in Julia's arm and the other end hooked up to a bottle beside the bed. The face under the tent was blurred and unfamiliar and very ill-looking. Blue veins stood out in her temples and her gold hair looked lifeless, and as she focused bright, feverish eyes on me, I was shocked at how sunken her cheeks had become. I didn't realize how sick she was and wished I hadn't come.

"Ana, you shouldn't be here," For the first time, I saw the figures of Julia's parents in the shadowy room.

"I just wanted to say hello," I said. My voice seemed to reverberate in the quiet room.

I looked at Julia. "I'm sorry I got mad at you, Julia. Just please, please get better."

I thought the thin face under the tent smiled, but I couldn't be sure.

I backed out of the room and into a furious starched nurse.

"What do you think you're doing? I could have you arrested. Not only are you under age, but the sign says "No Visitors". We have a case of bulbar polio here and it's contagious. Now get out!"

She crackled down the hall and I meekly followed.

As I pedalled home, I thought how old and scared Mrs. Podrowski looked today. Not at all like Blondie who sang that song and had rocked back and forth in her chair, laughing and begging my mother to "oh, please stop" when mama had teased her about Hubba Hubba Harry.

I didn't tell my mother about the visit, just scrubbed my hands and face although I hadn't touched anything, and left my shoes outdoors.

That evening, mama had all of us recite molitvi for Julia, and papa recited the Lord's Prayer, and I went to sleep, comforted.

That night, Julia died.

They hadn't had time to take her to Vancouver to put her in the iron lung.

"She might have been in the lung for months, even years," mama said. "This way she won't suffer. She's gone to heaven and is well now, and happy."

"How can she be happy when she's dead?" I said, "She was supposed to get better soon, and go back to school next term and we'd have sat together and lived in a duplex when we got married and I'd have babysat for her."

I ran outside, behind the woodshed where we'd sat the first time we'd met. I sat down on the boards and cried for Julia, the best friend I'd ever had.

Julia's parents took her body by train back to Saskatchewan to be buried, and never returned. Mother's cousin wrote to say she'd been to the funeral and Julia looked like a white angel in her organdy dress and baby doll shoes.

The neat, cool house under the maples was sold to a

noisy Italian family and when you walked by, you could hear singing and arguing, and smell tomatoes and garlic.

It was well into the summer holidays when mama brought out an envelope with "Findlay's Photo Shop" on it.

"Here are the May Day pictures, Ana," she said casually, handing me the envelope.

I flipped through the black and white pictures. Sara, Lisa and me in our costumes, my class dancing. And then Julia and I in our white dresses, smiling and squinting into the camera, arms around each other's shoulders.

I stared hard at Julia's face, wondering if somewhere she was watching me, if she was smiling her pale smile. Perhaps singing "We'll meet again someday, someday. Before the first of May."

"Oh my poor Blondie," my mother said, interrupting my thoughts. She was looking at a picture of Julia and her mother in front of the maypole, Mrs. Podrowski standing behind Julia, hands on her shoulders, smiling. "That's the way I always want to think of her ... happy."

And it occurred to me that my mother had her own songs to remember.

SUAD
Win
Crest